STARBURST

STEALING THE SUN: BOOK 2

RON COLLINS

SKYFOX
PUBLISHING
Science Fiction

STARBURST

STEALING THE SUN: BOOK 2

Cover Image:
© Philcold | Dreamstime.com

Skyfox Publishing

ISBN-10: 1-946176-02-8
ISBN-13: 978-1-946176-02-8

STEALING THE SUN

includes

STARFLIGHT

STARBURST

STARFALL

STARCLASH

STARBORN

Other Work by Ron Collins

Saga of the God-Touched Mage

includes

Glamour of the God-Touched
Target of the Orders
Trail of the Torean
Gathering of the God-Touched
Pawn of the Planewalker
Changing of the Guard
Lord of the Freeborn
Lords of Existence

Picasso's Cat & Other Stories

Five Magics

Six Days in May

Follow Ron at:
http://www.typosphere.com
Twitter: @roncollins13

For Dennis, again

Death is not the worst of evils.

General John Stark

CONTENTS

INTRODUCTION

When you have a full-course meal, the order of things matters. Appetizers are selected for specific purposes, and then you've got your palate cleansers and your entrees. The salad holds a specific place in things. As does dessert. Depending on the formality of it all, even the table setting carries its purpose and must be served just so.

An event like that is about the composite of the parts, and all the parts need to be in the right place to give them their proper due.

Against that idea, let me say that I've written several stories in series, and, for me, writing part two of anything carries its own set of challenges—the bulk of which are a lot like that.

I get concerned about basic continuity, of course, and I worry that the story needs to move along well. I want to knit it all together. It has to feel like the same world, but be fresh and interesting at the same time. Then you add in the simple human neurosis of not wanting to let anyone down. I mean, folks reading book two of anything are almost certainly doing so because part one worked for them—and therefore they come back to the world with expectations large enough that I can almost hear the "don't screw it up, Collins" whisper in the background as they crack open the first page.

But there's only so much I can do for those things.

The work will be the work in the end, and you guys will either like it or you won't.

For me, though, writing this set of books has been like putting together that full-course meal.

I touched on this a bit in the introduction of *Starflight*, the fact that the structure of this series is a little different than other multipart stories I've worked on. This story is built around characters who inhabit vastly different regions of our galaxy, who live their lives separated by light years of distance. So the telling of the whole isn't as linear as some others. And, the key word in that conversation is the word *character*.

I love these characters.

I want to do right by them.

I want to put them all into the right course.

So one of the challenges for me in developing this series was coming to the viewpoint that the stories were about the characters (quite surprising, eh?), and that this meant I had to structure the first three books in such a way as to give them extra breathing room (You get a story! You get a story! You get a story! he says, pointing at each character). I've had this entire saga in my head and in various forms of manuscript for a long time, but in the early days I put them together in ways that resulted in the whole of the books never quite working for me. The broccoli was always touching the potatoes, you know? (Yes, I'm stretching the metaphor, are you hungry yet?).

Then I started "talking to" my characters—or, more appropriately, started listening to them as they argued with me. Until then, many elements of the story that you now hold in your hand were scattered over several parts of the series. But once I gave each of these characters their own space—let them do their things in their own books—well, things started to feel right to me.

So the fact is that *Starburst* is completely what it is because the characters told me this is how it had to be. As usual, I think they were right.

Aside: a few years back a friend of mine asked if I ever got lonely writing (because, let's face it, creating words is a solitary task). I told her that since I had hundreds of characters running around in my head, I rarely felt truly lonely. She looked at me then, got one of those intriguingly amused expressions on her face, and said, "I might not tell certain other people that if I were you."

Heh.

Regardless, the structure of this book, and arguably the entire series then, is essentially a full-course meal that's been thrown together by my characters talking to me.

And, yes, I really do absolutely love these characters.

I hope you do, too.

Ron Collins
October 2016

On Human Pyramids & the Creation of Wormholes

The Birthday Story (Part 1)

Chang Park, Mare Imbrium, Luna
Local Solar Date: April 3, 2173
Local Solar Time: 1245 Hours

Casmir Francis leaned into the slide and crushed on the rush of power that rumbled through his pressure suit as the shimmy-pad skidded to a stop. A knifelike rooster tail of regolith fanned out against the black sky in a stellar display of low-g art. He was twenty-two and finally feeling good. Life was very, very fine.

Chang Park may be barren and gray, but sometimes barren and gray was pretty damned sharp. The park was a stark, nearly smooth plot of Lunar land that started about ten klicks from campus and ran all the way to the jagged peaks to the east. The makeshift rows of workstations his team had constructed last night were scattered along the southern pavilion, surrounded now by a growing gathering of students.

After months of planning, this was Pyramid Day—the day the United Government would see what his people could do. The day the Solar System would see what kind of statement his generation could make—what kind of people were going to break the stranglehold of the commercial branch of government and lead the Solar System into the future.

The park was safe enough that he didn't need to lock his shimmy-pad, so he just left it with the other couple hundred scooters, shimmies, and skimmers—their bodies ancient, dented, worn, and otherwise splattered with prismatic swirls and multi-d stickers that had been pasted fashionably into chaotically brilliant individual statements of the whole.

One read "42 or Bust." Another "Expand the Expanse!"

These are my people, he thought.

Casmir breathed the crisp air of his pressure suit and looked up into the deep darkness they were all standing under. The power of the universe pulsed through his entire being.

He couldn't keep the smile off his face.

The advance crew had pressed a pathway into the regolith to keep the dust and grit down. He crossed it, thrilling to the coarse rhythm that reverberated inside his helmet as his boots crunched over the surface. Even the taste of his saliva was sweet. The path wouldn't save him any effort cleaning his pressure suit, but it made running a bit easier so he bounced forward, enjoying the low-g movement while he could.

He felt incredible today, too—which was brilliant.

Cystic fibrosis was strange-assed condition, a disease with hundreds of variants that each required their own unique remedy. It was just his damned luck that even though half the damned CF world was cured, his variant was merely semitreatable. It was just a matter of time, though. That's what the doctors all told him whenever he went for examinations.

Just a matter of time.

Easy for them to say.

Living with CF meant a lot of things.

It meant always thinking about his diet. It meant taking the right pancreatic enzymes at the right times as he ate, and understanding the values of minerals like zinc and iron in ways most people never had to think about. He replaced his mucus thinner patch twice a day, and kept old-fashioned nebulizers with him at all times, just in case. And he could spot a possible home for festering bacteria from a hundred paces. Living with CF meant he could throw on a percussion vest in record time and practiced a variety of lung percussion techniques. He knew twenty-two different ways to cough that could help clear his lungs. At one point, Casmir had made a game of his coughing, calling them each by their own special name: The Baritone was deep and intentional; the Dignified

Dump was where he turned his head to the left, angled his jaw down, and tightened up just so.

At one point, Casmir considered a lung transplant, but his doctor didn't think it was time, yet, and he didn't want to deal with everything else that would mean.

All because of his cystic fibrosis.

In the end, living with this disease came down to the fact that he had to deal with never knowing what tomorrow meant. He dreaded things like calendar commitments and class schedules. Mostly things worked out, of course. Mostly he kept himself healthy by avoiding infections, staying away from places that screwed with the respiratory system, and exercising to keep his capacity strong.

But nothing was ever certain, and yesterday had been touch and go.

Between power-dosing antihistamine blocks and heroically failing to write his defense amid bouts of dozing, he spent most of the day worried his lungs wouldn't let him make it out here—which would have pissed him off in the hardest way possible. His mom said that having CF meant never having to say you're sorry, but that was the biggest piece of bullshit he could imagine. There was a good chance this pyramid would be a record: over a thousand blocks. Almost too big to imagine. If the record fell it might last forever. And everyone knew that a record like that would be impossible to ignore. If the record fell, only the hardest core of hard-core UG supporters could miss the message it would send.

Together we will rise up, their pyramid would say.

Together we will build the future.

He couldn't wait to see the United Government stewards choke out their commentary.

Given that he was graduating next month, this P-Day might also be his final shot—the last time he could be part of a real build.

To miss it would have crushed him.

He headed toward the mat, which was a film of roughened rubberized compound the size of a football field, carefully marked with each build station. The clock flickered at the corner of his display.

He didn't want to let Perigee down.

She would be late of course. But Perigee, the name Ellyn Parker performed under, was a diva. Her "entrances" were part of her thing, which meant they were part of what made everyone love her.

People would notice if *he* was late, though.

Ellyn would have his back, of course.

She had always had his back—even in the early days when the shit was particularly rough. He owed her more than he could ever really repay. And this was her time. With only a few weeks until graduation he wasn't going to cause her grief if he could help it, so he wanted to be on time.

He did a hop-and-skip run to the assignment station.

"Caz!" The voice came to his private channel.

"Hello, Jess," he replied.

Jess Igari was in the Social Policy department where Casmir was taking a political science major and a minor in business philosophy focused on Solar System structures. It was a pairing he explained as "I think, therefore I should be the hell in charge," which he considered hilarious but pretty much no one else seemed to get. Perhaps that said something about his sense of humor. Igari sharp enough, a year behind Casmir but having already served internships in the asteroid belt and on Io Station. He sat at a bench in his orange and blue pressure suit, waving a computer scanner at the dataskin interfaces on the pressure suits of students gathered around the table.

"Happy P-Day," Jess said to him.

"You too."

"I was afraid you wouldn't make it."

"I'm fine," Casmir replied, hiding his scowl. No one else needed to know that yesterday he could barely breathe on his own. He raised the back of his hand to show his dataskin. "You got my assignment?"

"E2," Jess said, pressing the scanner against the suit.

The assignment scrolled across his display. "Excellent!"

E2. Fifth slot over, second row up. Made sense. He exercised like his life depended on it, so he was as strong as a horse. The lower in the build, the better. Being a second rower was good, too, because that meant he represented the disenfranchised.

The base stood for the broken and disabled.

Row 2 was the disenfranchised, row 3 the working poor.

As the pyramid grew upward, each row represented those more well off before topping off with the ultras who had gotten so powerful after the Contraction that they almost shouldn't be there. He liked that he wasn't on the base, because he already represented the "disabled" as far as a lot of people were concerned, and he saw no reason to double down on that shit.

"Where do I get my shelves?" he said.

"See Preeti," Jess replied, pointing across the mat to where the organizers had set up the equipment shelters and the emergency air locks that were required anytime a lot of people gathered a distance from the protected atmosphere on LUMI's campus.

"Great," he replied.

"Have a good climb," Jess said as Casmir bounced away.

The Birthday Story (Part 2)

Casmir had loved Ellyn Parker since the day he first saw her, four years ago during orientation week.

She was in the student dome on Union Corner that day, performing dance poetry to the beat of an island percussionist while sporting dye-dark hair, a collage of face paint, and nails that flared with a rainbow of colors. She wore a yellow leotard programmed to flash phrases like *Ten Men Down*, which referred to the mines on Ceres, and *Save the Ice Cap*, regarding the Free Europa environmental movement—all of which marked her as overtly political, and all of which meant that she was the most intensely interesting person he had ever met.

A week later, at the end of his Intro to Poly Sci class, he suffered what his mother had long ago termed *an event*.

His lungs were full of crap that morning, and he had a searing pain in his lumbar. He was tired and listless from being up too late. He considered skipping but wanted to be a real student, and as his primary school football coach always told him, you can't play from the goddamned sideline. So when the coughing started, he did the Baritone and the Transcendental Huff, and he took his thinners and he ran the percussion vest for even longer than he normally would.

A half hour later he found himself in one of those mass sessions with some two hundred students smashed together, taught in the infamous LUMI-1 Dome.

At first his coughing drew only a few spurious glares, but he knew right away where it would end.

After a moment, space began to clear around him.

"Shut the hell up," an echoing voice said.

"Get away from him," another whispered. "He'll make us all sick."

Which was ridiculous.

CF isn't contagious, and he didn't even have an actual cold at the time. But fear is what fear does, and he found no lack of irony in the fact that since so many illnesses had been cured most people could go years without meeting anyone who was really sick. When they did, it was not unusual for them to get upset.

"Of course they would be afraid," his mother said when he was a kid. "You can't understand what you haven't seen." And on his better days, Casmir could even understand why people would be afraid of him. Hell, he was afraid of himself some days. This, however, was not one of his better days.

The lecture continued, but by the time he was hacking uncontrollably, the pack of students around him were in a panic.

"Why did they let the idiot in?"

"Go choke in the vacuum."

"Get the hell out of school."

Only Ellyn stepped forward to help him gather his shit up, lead him out the door, and help him to the medical center, where she stayed until the nurse came to get him.

"When can we talk again?" he said as she was preparing to leave.

She smiled with her perfectly white teeth and her perfectly smooth skin. He remembered she smelled like a flower.

"You can come to our next meeting," she said. "I'll send you the details."

Opening the message later, he saw the meeting was an open mic discussion focused on Lunar water rights and how they would set precedence for use on Europa—a topic he knew nothing about, but that suddenly held more interest than he could express.

He went and watched her work.

It was obvious Ellyn was brilliant in every way a person can be brilliant. She was tall, strong, breathtaking to the eyes, sharp-witted, and kind. She spoke her mind without being caustic, and she held to her positions even under wilting fire. Her politics were a strange goulash of socialism, capitalism, and a kind of moralism extracted from both pop culture and the more fervent religions of the Solar System. "Take the time to know you're right," she said, "then go ahead."

It was obvious that her core was the individual.

Her focus was you.

And when she thought something was right, you couldn't budge her.

It was also obvious that she was way out of his league.

Like everyone else on campus, though, that didn't stop him from falling completely in love with her.

The Birthday Story (Part 3)

"I need a pair of shelves," Casmir said to Preeti Indihari, pressing the dataskin to her assignment reader.

She stood behind a rickety table and clicked her gaze to a control button to mark him off a list she was maintaining. "Glad to see you could make it," she said. The radiation shield on her faceplate was engaged, but her dark eyes and rounded cheeks were still visible inside her helmet.

Like Jess, Preeti was a junior. The two of them would be leaders next year. They were good, but neither were anything like Ellyn.

She went to a pile and brought a pair of shelves forward. They were simple enough devices: padded, cylindrical things that strapped around his thighs, each about fifteen centimeters long with built-in platforms cast into each outer side. Every "block" would wear them to provide footholds to other blocks, who would then act as subsequent blocks for those in higher rows.

"Be strong," she said.

"Are you climbing today?" he replied.

"D22." The white of her teeth flashed behind her faceplate.

"You'll be a long way up and to my right."

"Another reason I want you to be strong."

Casmir chuckled and clamped the shelves onto his thighs, pulling a pair of straps until the shelves were tight enough to hold but not so tight as to constrict blood flow.

Across the field to the east, the mountainous ridges of the Sinus Iridium extension and the Caucasus peaks cut sharp, white-tipped paths against the black horizon. Venus hung low in the sky, but otherwise Earthlight dimmed the star pattern to the point that the dome above was almost pure black. Four temporary structures were built along the edge of the park—each with hundreds of participants mingling around them, students who were chatting in the public bands, almost certainly getting themselves all spun up about whatever issue was bothering them the most. The Martian ambassador's proposal to block a low-cost waypoint station on Phobos was the most popular bluster of the day.

Casmir didn't want to ruin things, though, so he kept off the public bands and just walked to his place on the mat. *Focus*, he thought. Today was about reversing the Contraction—turning back the page on the process by which all Earth governments, and then by definition most of the Solar System governments, gathered themselves up into a single entity.

The United Government wasn't even trying to hide the fact that they were a corporate shell now, a small group of political elites, bought and paid for by a big group of corporate elites, who controlled everything in the civilized Solar System.

It wasn't right.

Striding along, he felt the hair on the back of his neck bristle up.

People were literally starving, and no one cared because there was no cash flow in it to care. Casmir needed to be sure that the statement came out loud and strong. *Yes*, he thought. *That's what I want to be pissed off about today.*

A lot of planning had gone into this.

Reporters had been tipped off. News crews covered the lead-up to the protest and were now set up to give what Perigee called "Max-E," or Maximum Exposure. This was going to be huge. The number of protesters who turned out was amazing. Excitement was palpable.

He took his spot on the mat.

The safety pad—an air-filled buffer that would catch Perigee's fall—was already laid down. It was two meters tall and filled with gas from the cylinders the organizers had brought in. The compressor had been his idea. It saved transporting a huge air mattress on a skimmer, which would have been a pain in the ass.

The pad was positioned at what would be the center of a forty-two-row pyramid, but it was on a rudimentary pair of rails that made the target area adjustable out to fifty-five rows.

They were going for a record, no reason to skimp on optimism.

Adrenaline made his hands shake. He took a deep breath and marveled at the sense of freedom he got from the simple feeling of a pair of clear lungs. He could actually hear his heart beating.

The kickoff signal came as a green flash across his faceplate.

Basher Kline stood at E1, Frederic Proust at F1.

Casmir levered himself up, then straightened.

"I'm go for build," he said, with more professionalism than needed.

When the next row was in place, he braced his hands against the waists of the blocks above him.

"You good, Caz?" Basher said.

"I'm good," he replied. "Frederic?"

"I'm good," Frederic said.

The cycle was be repeated every sixty seconds. *Always think safety*. It was drilled into the group at every planning meeting.

The physics of the human pyramid said that it was possible to do as many as sixty rows before the angular momentum of the moon's rotation made the process unstable, but only if the members at the center were rock solid. No one had ever managed more than thirty-five rows before.

The pyramid grew out and to the right as the build continued.

Ten rows. Fifteen. Twenty.

Casmir sucked on water and tried to both relax and stay strong at the same time. His legs strained as the weight grew. The Lunar gravity helped, but mass was mass. Like compound interest, it all added up. His quads burned. Sweat poured over his body. Per the process, he rested his arms by releasing the block on his left for ten seconds, then the block on his right—giving each teammate a quick double squeeze to warn them before doing so.

A blue light flashed in his faceplate to remind him he represented the disenfranchised.

He opened his assigned frequency and spoke.

"I stand for people who cannot stand for themselves," he broadcast. "I stand for people who are not allowed to succeed."

Forty-five minutes into the build, the pyramid reached the previously magic number of thirty-five rows.

A record.

They had done it.

Rejoicing filled the public channel.

Then Ellyn appeared.

She rode on a platform pulled by a skimmer, holding onto a rail like a water-skier as the machine paraded her around. Her golden pressure suit was as blocky as any other pressure suit in existence, yet somehow still managed to cling to her in ways that made her photogenic. The skimmer edged around the group, finally stopping to let her salute them all as the pyramid continued to build.

He felt big then. He felt powerful. A tear ran down his cheek.

There was nothing his people could not accomplish.

The brine of his sweat tasted sharp as he stood at the base of the record-breaking pyramid. He took in the powdered gray regolith marked with thousands of footsteps, and he absorbed the black sky behind the ramshackle shelters his fellow students had built. A sense of the future came over him that was too much.

As Ellyn stepped off of the platform, Casmir opened the channel and said his chant for the disenfranchised again.

In many ways, Ellyn Parker was the most important person in his life. She had changed who he was, made him into someone who saw possibilities rather than barriers. Watching her leave the skimmer, he imagined the news reports about her tomorrow. She was the beautiful one, speaking out against the United Government and its ugly Contraction with a total lack of fear.

In just a few moments, Ellyn would climb to the top row and make her statement. Then she would let herself fall gracefully to the surface where the air mattress would catch her. Even under the moon's gravity, a fall from that kind of height could wind up all sorts of bad. But that wouldn't happen today because they had it planned out, and because Ellyn Parker was here leading them. She wouldn't let them fail. Then the pyramid would break itself down, and the partying would begin.

"You good?" It was Basher again.

His legs ached now. Sweat was pooling in the joints of his suit and he felt the calcium grind of pressure on his knees. But Casmir knew he could stay like this forever if he needed to.

"I'm good," he replied.

"I'm good," Frederic added, his voice straining, too.

Perigee stood at the base of the pyramid and spoke into the public channel.

"With this tower of compassion, we ask our fellow human beings to wake up! Be aware of what the system is doing to us! As I climb across the backs of the broken and disabled who cannot fend for themselves, and as I tread upon the disenfranchised, the poor, the working class who are struggling to find the simple freedoms that only those at the top of the pyramid can give, we in Universe Three say that no group of people can control us if we do not wish to be controlled. To our fellow humans, we say stand up! Climb us! Be one with us!"

With that Perigee lowered her visor and began a climb she did blind in order to represent the nature of leadership. She rose steadily, using deliberate motions that gave the pyramid time to progress farther right and farther upward.

The private channel called out Ellyn's progress.

"V5 shoulder firm," a voice called.

"U6 thigh confirmed," another followed.

"V6 shoulder good."

The build was forty rows and still growing. He wanted to see the video, but knew that no picture would be better than what he was imagining—the pyramid, tall and majestic in the sunlight, glimmering with an almost prismatic spectrum of reflected pressure suits that looked like a gossamer shark fin as it rose up from an ocean of regolith.

The temporary shelters ahead of him looked vacant and lonely now.

The tables stood silent sentry. A few unused sets of shelves lay in a scattered pile next to the makeshift storage bin.

At first they were just three silver dots on the horizon.

Clippers, small spacecraft with antigrav hover engines configured for Lunar operations, were running at high speed and coming straight for Chang Park. Casmir's initial thought was that they were journalists. He was so sure of this he clicked the private channel to report the story was going extra-Lunar.

Then it struck him.

Other than the safety center, the grounds were completely empty.

The reporters had left. Without a word, the news channels had retreated. There would be no video. No recording. Truth hit him like a cold shower from inside his skin. These clippers were not journalists. As the three craft came closer, Casmir saw they were official vehicles, sharp-edged and solid, Engagement class clippers that cut through space like shivs.

All of them carried the UG flag.

The first clipper hit the center of the formation about two-thirds of the way up, scattering bodies all directions and causing a warping ripple in the pyramid. The second hit about a third of the way up. The third circled as blocks fell, watching the execution of the mission and almost certainly capturing the events for a report— or at least ready to capture a report if the mission had not been carried out as ordered.

The public channel erupted with screaming voices and calls for help.

Parts of the formation that hadn't been attacked began to disband, blocks sliding down each other's backs in a panicked cascade, bodies tumbling down, hands whipping back and forth in vain attempts to halt their falls.

Oblivious to their calls, the two clippers turned and made another pass.

PROLOGUE

UGIS *Everguard*
Ship Local Date: May 7, 2204
Ship Local Time: 1200 Hours

4.3 light years away from the Solar System, three waves of highly sophisticated pods flew into the outer reaches of Alpha Centauri A's corona. Their motors drove themselves down through its solar atmosphere, injecting themselves into the heat of its chromosphere and continuing deeper, rushing toward the true core of the star to find the fusing mass of helium and hydrogen that formed its life. Laminated layers of bioactive composite and nanointelligent titanium that had been designed to withstand the six-million-degree core worked together to shed heat.

Four pods came in the first wave.

Four more in the second.

Only three in the third.

The scientists who built them had created models of the star using information gleaned from their own sun. It was a G2-type star, rotating in twenty-two days rather than Sol's twenty-five. It was bigger than Sol, but only by a little. It had higher metal content, a factor that caused the scientists to make several changes to the bioactive components of the heat shield. They made assumptions about density, gravity, and the impact of rotational velocity and the angular momentum of the material that sluiced inside the star. They made learned estimates about the surface pressure that material would put on the outer shells of the pods, and about the thermal gradient the pods would pass through as they made their way to the star's radiative zone and into the core itself.

One of the pods failed upon entry into the corona.

The rest found their designated moment, communicated with each other through quantum-linked connections, and engaged the last lines of their coded mission.

Wormhole actuators engaged.

Energy flowed, hydrogen fusing to helium.

Dimensions twisted. Mathematics screamed. The pods themselves disintegrated to instant ash, adding their atomic makeup to Alpha Centauri A's metalicity while, inside the star, the compressed fabric of time and space tore itself apart with an explosion that would show up as a single pulse of brightness that passed through the Solar System's astronomical instruments nearly four and a half years later.

When it was over, the star was quiet.

Alpha Centauri A had a new feature—a jump gate buried deep inside.

For all the sophistication it took to build it, the gate was simplistic in its stature now, a "multi-gate" as the scientists called it, a simple connection that could be linked to by any other device that knew the quantum key of its creation.

To the people who created it, however, the issues around it were more complex.

It was a multi-gate, yes.

But it was a multi-gate that could change at least two worlds, and maybe more.

On Space Clippers, and Messages From Deep Space

Chapter 1

The rover-sled lurched over the Martian landscape as Casmir's daughter brought it to an abrupt halt.

"Nice job," he said. "Tomorrow maybe we assign you to the bot drivers."

"Sorry," Deidra replied, her cheeks coloring with embarrassment for the rough stop.

The vehicle was a simple two-seater with a storage compartment for expeditions, something easy for her to start with. Its motor wound down and the vehicle bounced to the ground amid a cloud of orange dust. Outside, the rising sun was strong enough to cut through the butterscotchy clouds and cast a black shadow over the hill ahead of them.

"Come on," she said.

"Slow down," Casmir said. "The UG will be watching."

"Let them," she said. "I look good today."

He glared. *Thirteen years old*, he thought.

Casmir flicked his visor down and toggled its optical control to lock the seal. The sled's environmental controllers registered its containment and let Deidra open the cockpit doors. She was on the surface before Casmir said he was ready to go.

He gave a hard cough that sounded like a damned earthquake inside his suit. His daughter, like his two sons, was a miracle for someone like him. He understood that more and more as the years passed. CF robbed a person of their strength. When he was sick, he couldn't breathe and he had pains that were impossible to describe. It also robbed men of their ability to reproduce—usually, anyway. When they decided to have children, he had done all the testing, and worked with the genetic doctors to guard against him passing the gene sequence that caused his version of the disease, but nothing was guaranteed yet. Like most men with CF, he had other issues, too. His doctors had harvested his sperm, and they had made babies the remote way. Not particularly sexy, he supposed, but watching his daughter bounce over the Martian surface made him happy he lived at a time when such practices were there for him.

As usual for this day, he thought about Ellyn Parker as he slid his legs over the running board. It was over thirty years ago she died. Long enough that he'd lived on two planets, eight moons, and a couple dozen asteroids. Long enough that he'd lost friends. Long enough that he'd won a hundred battles against the UG, and yet—despite victories—the United Government and the companies behind it were bigger today than they had ever been. He was tired and worn down this time, getting to be an old man—fifty-four now, but fifty-four for him was probably like a hundred-four for the average bum. The years of fighting had been long enough to grind whatever idealistic enthusiasm he once had down to a stub of simple practicality.

What would Ellyn think of them if she were here?

He hoped she would be proud, but he was no longer sure.

On young legs, Deidra ran ahead to the foothills of the formation.

"Come on, Papa! I'm beating you!"

He thought about warning her against UG surveillance again, but though she was the youngest of his children, she already understood that aspect of their lives better than the rest. As long as she stayed on this side of the hill she should be fine.

He leaned on his walking staff, and coughed up phlegm again. The weight of his custom suit made it feel like he was walking through water. The surface of the planet bent to brown at his periphery outside a faceplate that misted over with each breath. Vital signs glowed on his display: blood oxygen on the low end of "still living," heart rate pounding at one-forty, pressure on the embarrassingly high side—but good enough, goddammit, good enough despite the scowl on Yvonne's face as she took the readings this morning. He'd barely been on the surface for a minute and already his knees were screaming. His lower back was on slow burn, and every time he took a breath, pain raked his ribs.

He stopped to arch his back again.

The suit's ventilation system cleared his faceplate, but the supply of fresh air was too dry. He sucked water from the reservoir. It tasted like plastic, but it helped cut the burn everywhere except his nasal passages, which still felt like he was sucking on razors every time he breathed. Just the thought made him cough again, so he swallowed more water.

"That's all right," Casmir replied. "You go ahead."

He and Yvonne had decided to shield their children from certain realities until they were old enough to understand them.

They both watched everything as closely as they could. They both blocked news and both set penalties. Yvonne handled the schooling herself. But information is a bitch, there are limits to what can be controlled, and their kids weren't stupid. Wallace and Cash picked up things by accident, and put the bits together just fine. But Deidra was a natural sleuth, pure and simple. She knew how to dig. As such, Casmir and Yvonne decided their children would learn everything at thirteen standard years old.

"Papa!"

Deidra was already at the top of the hill.

"Hold your rockets, little one," he called, suppressing another cough.

He took another glance at the sky.

The weather had been stagnant for long enough that Casmir wouldn't cry if it kicked up one of those dust storms that left people talking for days afterward. A storm like that could be a pain in the ass, but afterward the air would be filled with sheets of ice crystals and particles of magnetite, hematite, and any other mineral the atmosphere could pick up and hold.

During the morning hours those particles caught the sun to make gauzy drapes of purple and blue. At nighttime, though, for just those few moments after the sun set, light bending from under the horizon would reflect off the thinnest layers of the atmosphere to catch those crystals and those flakes of minerals, and it would turn them into jaw-dropping rivers of silver and blue that burned like a prismatic fire against the backdrop of stars.

Yvonne called them silver bows, but he preferred to leave them nameless so he could think of them as some kind of magic.

These were the kinds of things that kept Casmir fighting. They reminded him that, despite pain, life was beautiful.

He looked to where the Alpha Centauri system would be visible if it wasn't daytime. If the *Everguard* mission was both successful and on schedule, the UG's new Star Drive spacecraft could achieve faster-than-light travel any time now. The idea depressed him. No matter how beautiful the world, or how noble the act of living on it, Casmir didn't know if he could fight that kind of power.

"I'm on my way," he said, pushing himself up the hill.

Yes, he was tired, but his daughter was waiting and it was her thirteenth birthday.

CHAPTER 2

Perigee Hill: Mars Colony Divide
Local Solar Date: February 12, 2206
Local Solar Time: 0855 Hours

Casmir made it to the ridge to see his daughter gazing over the landscape. The United Government's Mars Colony Natim complex was spread out before her.

"It's pretty," Deidra said.

"I suppose it is," he replied, sitting on a flat rock so he could catch his breath. "In its own way."

The UG complex covered the northern edge of the slope. Its network of plastiglass domes and rounded tubes made it look like a galactic hamster's wet dream. Black and silver antenna rose like prickly pear, and a wafting cloud of beige steam clung to the central power station.

Clippers hovering among the buildings made Casmir grit his teeth.

They were armed pods filled with law enforcement people assigned to patrol the grounds under the guise of protection, though *protection* in this case meant *compliance* and a shield against illegal import/export.

Above them, in Low Mars Orbit, a network of twelve S-class electronic intelligence satellites would be following them. The trackers probably couldn't ID either him or Deidra, but since they followed every Universe Three surface operation no matter how small, he was certain they had surveillance company.

"They look different in person," Deidra said, staring at the stark white clippers. "Will the Uglies come after us?"

"Only if they think they can get away with it." Casmir let the use of her slang pass. He didn't mind the idea of it, but he didn't like the word itself. He didn't like how that lumped everyone together and that it belittled the power of the UG, but he understood its humor.

"What does that mean?"

He shrugged and grimaced under his faceplate. The UG police would harass them if they could, but it was a tough game for them right now. Businesses liked civilization to be stable. Violence, especially unprovoked violence, futzed with the currency pipelines those businesses had so carefully laid across the Solar System. Casmir worked hard to see that Universe Three's activity always stuck in the UG's craw, but he was also careful to avoid going so far that the UG could be justified in blatantly attacking their outposts.

Ignoring the occasional dustup or deep-space riot, it worked well enough. Of course, if the UG knew it was "the" Casmir Francis and his daughter sitting here today, it would cause a clutching of hearts and a scrambling of squadrons that would be humorous to watch if it wasn't so dangerous.

He wanted her to understand that, but it was too much for her now. He needed to introduce her to the idea that their world was different from what she thought it was first. The time for such complexities would come.

"We'll discuss that later."

"Tell me the birthday story, Papa. I want to hear it."

"I will. But we need to talk about a few other things first."

She waited.

"You see the greenhouses?" he said, pointing to rows of glass-walled buildings constructed low to the ground and lined with individual solar panels.

"They look like dominoes," she said.

"They do, don't they? But what they actually are is home to the UG's Martian agricultural program."

"Their farm?"

"Yes," he said, smiling to himself.

Deidra was a brilliant young girl, but she was still a young girl. He had to remember to speak in simpler terms.

"Inside that farm is the UG's latest attempt to grow genetically designed crops that can survive in the open Martian atmosphere."

"Like fields on Earth?"

"Uh-huh," Casmir confirmed.

Her sigh was an audible expression of disappointment that matched the deflation in her body language. "That's not going to work," she said.

"No, it won't," Casmir replied, knowing he didn't have to explain exactly why the effort was doomed to fail.

The arrogant bastards were trying to convert a predominantly CO_2-laced atmosphere into one of nitrogen and oxygen using terraforming concepts that were outdated even a century ago. Even if vegetation alone could ever provide the cleansing they needed, there were soil issues and radiation effects to deal with, both of which would take trillions of solar dollars and decades of time to overcome. And those were just the first of the hurdles the UG was pretending they could leap past as they made Mars sustainable.

He flexed his hands. His circulation was for shit these days and his fingers ached with cold inside his gloves. The suit regulated his body temperature, but it didn't do anything for his circulation, something that made it harder to forget that the temperature outside was fifty-eight below zero—another little problem for UG's ag engineers to waste a few billion solars on.

"It won't work, but still the UG has built these dominoes," he said. "Do you know why?"

"No," she replied.

Her attention was diverted by a clipper that turned toward them, then back on its preprogrammed profile. Casmir watched his daughter's body language as she tensed and relaxed. He was glad she was worried. You should never trust the UG.

"Why are they doing that?"

"To understand the UG, you have to see how solar dollars flow for the companies that run it. When you do that, you see that the UG is more interested in commerce than in progress."

"Don't the two go together?"

"Sometimes, yes. But not always. For example, what do you

think happens when the government makes it possible for companies to make money while doing research and scientific studies regardless of whether those studies are successful—and that, in fact, failed experiments are in many ways more profitable than successful research?"

He remained silent, interested to see how Deidra processed the idea he had just given her.

"Every time they fail they get to start a new project?"

"I'm glad you can see that."

Then he went on a coughing jag hard enough that he wished he was back home. It was definitely time to see Dr. Iwal.

"Are you all right?" Deidra said, turning to him.

"I'm fine."

He took a drink and cleared his throat.

"You were correct, though. Each *failure* breeds new scientific efforts that can be funded through the government—which means through taxing the people—whereas a *success* moves the project further out of the realm of pure science and into production, which eventually turns the result into a commodity—at which point profit is sustainable based merely on the marketplace rather than the grossly obscene pile that comes on demand from the government."

"It's a big money pump," Deidra said.

Casmir laughed. "Yes, it is. And it means progress comes only at the pace with which industry needs it to keep the people happy and occupied enough to keep tax solars flowing."

He could almost see her frown. It would take a while for the complexity of the system to settle on her, but he could see it happening already.

"Compare their approach to agriculture with our own," he said, motioning to the greenhouses.

"We grow our food down in Mushroom Canyon."

She referred to the underground stations Universe Three had built years ago, where their botanists had developed a sustainable form of farming based on molds, recirculating fertilization, and strictly controlled environments. The resulting cuisine was sometimes less than attractive, but was quite easily sustainable within the colony itself if they could not trade for other food that was more exciting.

"It's not as beautiful as fields of grain," he said. "But while UG bureaucrats try to create their lines of corn that fade into the orange horizon, and while their farming industry spends trillions of solar dollars selling the idea of new markets to these same bureaucrats, our approach frees resources to focus on more valuable ideas."

Deidra came closer, and her helmet reflected a fish-eye image of the Universe Three side of the divide.

The landscape there lay like a stone tapestry, scarred and broken with crevasses and a pair of small observation domes but otherwise barren and natural under the bright, uniform sky. A patch of ice flared in the distance.

He always loved the starkness of the Martian horizon.

"Is it not beautiful there, too?" he said to her.

"It is," Deidra said. "But it's different."

"How so?"

"It's so…jab."

"Jab," Casmir replied. "Indeed."

He let his gaze linger on the image in Deidra's faceplate.

The outline of his daughter's unlined face under the image that splayed across the visor gave him a flush of connection.

His people lived under the Martian crust that served to protect them from the harsh climate. They called their quarters the Hive, which he liked for both the physical image the word brought him and the essence of community it contained. It meant togetherness. It meant sacrificing for a culture. The name made him feel like his people enjoyed the sense of being one without the coercion of UG's clippers hovering just outside their dome.

Deidra took three steps to stand before him.

"I'm ready, Papa," she said. "Tell me the story."

Inside his helmet, he smiled.

Yes, he thought. *She's ready.*

CHAPTER 3

Perigee Hill: Mars Colony Divide
Local Solar Date: February 12, 2206
Local Solar Time: 0900 Hours

"Come on, Papa," Deidra said, standing with her arms crossed and her back arched—classic Deidra. "You told it to Cash and to Wallace."

"Yes, I did," he groused. "But they were quiet about it."

The edge to her gaze was visible even beneath the sheen of her faceplate. She was stronger than her brothers. Deidra had the fire inside.

"This is the last time I get to tell the story, so I'm going to enjoy it."

Her glare burned through her faceplate.

Down in the colony, one of the clippers made a considerably wider turn than usual. Casmir wondered what the pilot had seen to cause the deviation. Was it them? Was it movement elsewhere?

"I wish I could see the clipper pilot's face," he said when the clipper returned to its usual cycle.

"Don't change the topic."

"In a strange way that was the beginning of the story."

"I don't see how."

"That's where your patience has to come to play. Come. Sit." He patted the flat rock beside him.

She huffed, but sat down.

"Today," he said, "I am going to tell you how we came to live on Mars."

"I already know where we came from."

"That is true. But I misspoke to a degree. This is a story about how we came to live *as* we do rather than how we came to live *where* we do. But I will begin with the fact that when I was a boy, I lived in a place called England." He pointed to the sky. "If it weren't for the atmosphere, it would be a very bright spot right there."

"I know where the Earth is."

Casmir chuckled.

"But then Grandpapa picked you up and moved you to Luna," she said.

"That's right. Just like we move sometimes, but different. Companies were just beginning to figure out how to do Lunar commerce then, and it was a busy time. Your grandpapa built things, and they needed people like him. We lived in caves a lot like the tunnels we live in now, but colder. We didn't have good radiation protection back then, either, so for the first few years only the workers were allowed on the surface."

"That's where you went to school."

"Yes. Eventually, we moved to surface domes. The college I went to—Lunar University: Mare Imbrium—was one of the first. And it was while I was just starting there at LUMI that all of the independent governments of Earth did a very dangerous thing."

"They Contracted."

Casmir appraised his daughter. How much did she already know? "That makes it sound like a good thing, doesn't it? Contracting?"

"Sounds smaller."

"Yes. Like the government is getting less powerful. And a less powerful government sounds like it should be good. More freedom for people, right?"

"Sure."

"But what happened in this case is that all the businesses came together and drove the governments into a single group because that is what all those businesses needed to happen."

"Why?"

"Why do *you* think?"

He waited.

"Easier to control."

"Sounds right to me, eh?"

"So," Deidra said. "One government got very big and the rest just went away?"

"Yes, exactly," Casmir said.

"Why wouldn't they just say it like that?" She held her hands up in mock confusion.

He shrugged.

The conversation was settling into a familiar flow, him laying out facts and letting her come to her own conclusions or ask her own questions, then pointing those conclusions or questions in directions he thought they were best pointed.

He had built Universe Three using this technique.

It was like a verbal martial art, using the conversation's momentum to shape itself into positions that were intuitive and natural. He was comfortable with it, and he enjoyed the sense of control that came from its practice. He liked helping people see things in new ways. Being persuasive like this was, perhaps, the only thing he was really good at.

"I don't know why people don't say what they mean, Deidra," he replied. "But that is how most people, and all politicians, speak. They tell you only the parts they think you need to know, so you must learn how to be careful when you listen to them."

He could imagine her chewing the inside of her cheek.

"Including you?"

"Yes, I suppose so. I'm a politician, so I'm dangerous. But I'm also your father, so that's different."

"Why?"

He heard the grin on her voice.

"Because it is," he said. "Suppose you tell me why this Contraction was so dangerous?"

"Because it meant there was only one way?"

"That's right—at least partially, anyway. It also meant that when they adjusted the rules—which they did often—they were able to adjust them in their own favor."

"But doesn't everyone vote?"

"Of course. The UG is still something of a democracy, but you, of all people, know exactly how easy it is to connive and twist things to get your own way, right?"

"I don't know what you mean," Deidra replied, her voice giving her away. His daughter had her brothers tied around her little finger, and everyone in the command center, including Deidra, knew it.

"I'm sure you don't," Casmir said, patting her knee. "But you, my lovely and intelligent daughter, get away with it because your brothers love you." He paused for effect. "The UG gets away with it because they play a majority-rules game, and they've learned that most people don't mind being told what to think as long as they believe they are getting what they want."

"Is that what you meant when you said it's easier to lead a person who thinks they're free than to tell that same person they're actually wearing chains?"

"You've been reading my talks."

"Maybe," she replied. "Is that what you meant?"

"Yes, that's what I meant. Politicians, and companies for that matter, learned long ago that the public is generally happy to go along with about anything as long as most of them don't feel threatened."

Casmir coughed.

He was getting tired. They would have to be going soon.

"It's important to understand that when a group controls something, they own it." He pointed to the vapor hanging over the UG's complex. "Take, for example, that power grid. The UG knows energy is the most important thing we need to survive. They can't cut us off or the press would destroy them. So, instead, they tell us how much we can use."

"That's why the lights go out at nine?"

"That's why the lights go out at nine on *our* side of the divide. They never go out on their side."

"That's not fair." Her voice gained an edge of anger. They were getting into fresh ground. This was the first time she understood that the Hive was under artificial rationing.

"No," he replied. "It's not fair."

"Why would they do that?"

"Because we don't blindly follow their wishes."

Deidra's sigh was calculating. "I don't understand."

"Let me tell you the rest of the story—the real story about how and when Universe Three was fully created—and see if it helps."

"All right."

Casmir began to speak, and as he put word against word, his mind faded back to the day when it began. The emotions, despite their age, felt fresh. The images of the events came back to him in crisp detail.

As it was when he first told Wallace, and again as he told Cash, telling his daughter the story of Perigee made him feel as if he was living it all over again.

Chapter 4

Perigee Hill: Mars Colony Divide
Local Solar Date: February 12, 2206
Local Solar Time: 0910 Hours

Deidra listened with an intensity that told Casmir she felt the story's importance.

She chuckled when he described the idea of the human pyramid.

"Sounds silly," she said.

"We were young," Casmir replied. "It meant something to us then."

She gasped when he described the attack, and the UG clipper crashing into the pyramid.

"That's, what, forty-five meters? Fifty? That's like the people at the top fell almost three stories on the Earth," she said. "Maybe six here on Mars."

"I didn't realize you were so adroit with numbers," he replied.

"Well," Deidra said primly. "You travel too much."

He nodded.

"The final count was forty-three dead. Several hundred more hurt. Being on the second row I was lucky. My suit was hardly damaged. But Perigee…even in the moon's gravity…I remember seeing her body," he said. "The crimson of her blood as it spread over the regolith, how it became nearly pink at the edges."

"Tell me about her," Deidra said after a moment. "Tell me

about Ellyn Parker."

He liked that. Neither Wallace nor Cash had asked about her, but he had known Deidra would.

"She called herself Perigee because she said people spent their lives circling around what was real, and she wanted to be as close to that truth as she could possibly get."

"A perigee is when a moon comes closest to its planet," Deidra said.

"Exactly," Casmir said. "She was brilliant. Very strong. Her parents were not good with her, but she learned how to live on her own when she was young. She was one of the first people I met who ever treated me like a regular person."

"Was she your girlfriend?"

"No," Casmir responded. "Everyone loved her, of course. But she was her own woman."

"Why did the UG clipper crash into the pyramid? Was it a mistake?"

"No, Deidra. It was no mistake. That's what they will want you to believe, though. Always. Every time something like this happens, they will say it was some kind of terrible mistake—a renegade officer gone wrong or a single person who made a terribly regrettable error in judgment. But it was no coincidence that the clippers waited until Ellyn was at her apex. They learned of our plans and they designed their attack. We all knew it, and we all knew why."

"Why?"

"Because one of her strongest ideas was that the government should keep its mitts off anyone unless that person was impeding someone else's ability to live their life well."

"Everyone *should* be free to do what they want as long as they aren't hurting anyone else," Deidra snapped.

Casmir patted her knee. "That should be true," he said. "But it isn't. Or, it can't be. People can't help but hurt other people, almost no matter what they do. Ellyn's view was actually quite different because she argued the flipside to that discussion was that when a person *did* impede someone else's life in a way that was 'inappropriate,' it was the government's job to see there were penalties, and she ran into trouble because she was talking about how all the companies that ran the government through their strawman connections were violating that basic principle merely by managing that 'money pump,' as you called it, to their own interests."

"She was attacking the companies?"

He grunted agreement. "Ellyn had been protesting their lockdown on private space exploration and their strict commandeering of resources at the time of the pyramid."

"Like the power systems?" Deidra said, staring at the complex.

"Exactly like the power systems," Casmir said.

"Ellyn cost them money."

"We didn't see it as clearly at the time, but she was telling the government they had to crack down on the companies' ability to dictate the flow of money. And by the time the event happened, people were listening too much. She had to be stopped."

Deidra thought about that, but didn't say anything.

"In retrospect, that day was the turning point of my life—as well, then, of yours."

"Why do you say that?"

"Because Universe Three didn't die when the government killed Ellyn. Instead, when news of the attack happened we brought in more people. We got stronger."

"How?"

He told her then about how he had taken the reins.

How he took Ellyn's framework, a system of three spheres—the Solar System, their galaxy, and the universe that consisted of all galaxies—and developed Universe Three beyond anything she would have envisioned. How he used Ellyn's views to keep Universe Three focused on keeping human beings free to roam them all. He explained his views of how greed and conglomerations were suppressive and would always be so. He talked about meeting Gregor Anderson who became his second in command, about fighting the UG on Luna before leapfrogging to Mars, and then Europa, and eventually to Io and the asteroid belt. He told Deidra about meeting her mother and how Yvonne advocated for all the real work that happened in the mines on Europa. He described successes and failures. He explained he had been put in prison for three weeks on Io when the UG was first creating a post there, and he finished by describing the months of effort it took to build the Hive.

***

When he was done, he took a drink of water and watched the clippers circle the UG complex. Was it his imagination, or were they growing in number?

He pressed his lips together.

"So, you're the leader?" Deidra said. "You decide what Universe Three is going to do?"

"I coordinate our plans. But yes, I drive decisions."

"Holy…" Deidra turned back to look at the UG complex. It wasn't often he could stand Deidra on her ear. "That's jab," she said.

"Very jab."

"I want to be like Perigee."

"That doesn't surprise me."

"I can't believe they killed her."

"I've told you and your brothers this story because I want you to understand who the United Government is. I want you to know they aren't actually evil so much as…limited. They believe in themselves and they believe in order. They will do what it takes to keep the system stable even if that stability means a third of the people in the Solar System can't live well, and they succeed because most people would rather not deal with facts that make them uncomfortable."

Deidra was silent for a long time. Just sat there, swaying with agreement.

"Why do *you* do it?" she said.

"What do you mean?"

"Perigee wanted to change how civilization worked."

"Yes."

"Is that what you want?"

Casmir turned to her, examining the lines of her jaw and cheekbones under her faceplate as closely as he could. *Yes*, he thought. *Deidra is the one*. She had absorbed the story. She understood the relationship between Universe Three and the United Government—or at least that there was one.

"I used to think exactly like Ellyn thought."

"And now you don't."

"I used to think that exposing hypocrisy alone would drive people to make changes themselves. But now I think the system is

40

like this disease I carry around inside me: Once you have it, you can't get rid of it. So the best thing is to never get the disease in the first place."

"Hmmmm."

"So…" He searched for words. "We fight the UG on the fringes now. We spend time on the frontier moons like Io and Europa, and we have people in the scatterings of the asteroid belt. Sure, we do what we can on Earth and Luna, and even the colonists here on Mars. But it's the frontiers where we can create the kinds of worlds we want to live in."

"So you want to keep the Uglies from growing?"

"We want to create new worlds where people can grow up without commercial oppression." He put his hands on his knees. "There is too much suffering, Deidra. Too much pain in the people who are not in the circle. I do this because I can't abide to live where people can't all have what they need."

She nodded.

"So, we still want exactly what Ellyn wanted, but you are right to sense that we've broken from her tactics. That's another reason I'm telling you this story. I want you to know that the changes your mother and I work for are not always about words."

"Not about words?"

"By that I mean we are more active than Ellyn would have been. We've given up trying to sway public opinion of the masses, and now we bring people to our side by deeds. And that means—if we are not very careful—we can put ourselves at great risk."

"I see," Deidra said. "So, does the UG know the Hive is your command post?"

He smiled.

"They know we are often here," he said, grabbing his walking stick and rising to stretch his cranky knees. He scanned the complex and saw that, yes, the clippers were gathering. It was time to get home. "But that is a discussion we can have later. Right now we have birthday cake to eat."

"And presents to open," Deidra said, also standing. "Don't forget the presents."

"No, no," Casmir said. "We mustn't forget the presents."

Chapter 5

Perigee Hill: Mars Colony Divide
Local Solar Date: February 12, 2206
Local Solar Time: 0945 Hours

The rover-sled was just as they left it, doors winged open, seat belts dangling across the running board.

"I'll drive again?" Deidra said as they approached. She had stayed closer to Casmir this time, helping him with his footing as he made it down the slope, a task that was always harder than climbing.

"Of course," he replied.

He was tired anyway. The EVA had taken more out of him than he wanted to admit, and now all he really wanted to do was to get home, sit down, and slap about twenty C-Pak doses onto his arm. Not that Yvonne would be happy with anything short of a trip to sick bay. He leaned against his walking stick, feeling the grind in his left knee the most.

He didn't notice the problem until they were almost upon it.

Footsteps.

Hastily erased.

But now that he saw them, Casmir saw they led to, or from, a rocky break in the mounded hills, coming from around a break where he was now certain he would find a parked clipper.

"Stop," he said to Deidra as she stepped around the front of the rover-sled toward the driver's entry.

But it was too late.

Two figures rose from where they had been hidden in the storage compartment. They were UG officers, their suits dark orange and blue and their antiradiation face screens glowing with an electrified golden sheen. They were armed and shielded, their plasma rifles short and stubby against their hips but pointed directly at Deidra and Casmir. Upon their appearance, two more came from around the point where Casmir assumed their clipper was docked.

To her credit, Deidra stopped and dropped her radio to the public frequencies, just as his operatives were trained to do. She stood still, her eyes growing wide as two officers detained her.

"We have visitors," Casmir said through his encrypted channel, then also dropped to the public.

One of the officers, a male, large, came toward him and waved his gun in the normal gung-ho style of a man too big for his gravity shoes. Utilities hung from his suit, and his arms ran with readout from what Casmir assumed was a network of communications sensors.

Casmir toggled a suppressor feature that would randomly alter the tonal aspect of his voice in case the officers were attempting to establish ID by vocal pattern matching.

Rule 4: Talk your way out if at all possible.

"What can we do for you?" he said. He stood taller and held onto his walking staff, knowing exactly how useless it would be in this kind of fight.

"ID?"

"My daughter and I are with the Hive, officer. Just out visiting the hill." He held one hand out to her. There was no way that letting these officers know who he was would end well. "You can see we're unarmed. We hold no false intentions here." Code in his suit activated, registering the frequency of the officer's communication and scanning Casmir's optical input at a resolution that his own eyes could never really pick out. The code flashed a series of lights and symbols as it traced and then acquired the networked paths between the four officers.

"I said, ID." The officer held up an arm with a datapad interface on it and waited for Casmir to proffer his.

Casmir nodded and sighed. "All right," he said. "Give it a moment to respond."

Rule 6: Act quickly.

Code loaded the protocol driver as he turned his inner arm to the officer.

The UG man held the plasma rifle close as he brought his reader in contact with the interface.

The instant he felt pressure, Casmir cracked his staff hard against the officer's knee. The man went down before he could fire a shot, then his entire body went slack.

The others, too.

"Get in," he said to Deidra without taking time to change the frequency.

She stood frozen in place, gazing at the two comatose officers now lying as motionless on the ground before her as the two that had been detaining Casmir. The code had worked, flashing its way into the direct links between the four to enable an injection of the emergency dose of anesthesia that officers and soldiers carried to kill pain in case of traumatic injury. The officers were conscious, but unable to function.

Casmir and Deidra had maybe five minutes.

He flipped encryption on.

"I said get in!" he said as adrenaline kicked in, and he ran the last four steps to the rover-sled, threw his staff into the back, hopped into the cab, and slid over to the seat.

"I thought I was going to drive," Deidra yelled.

"Get in," Casmir replied, his voice already steadying.

He put the antigrav toggle into gear as Deidra ran to the passenger slot, and he punched the door command to get the compartment sealed. The sled's motors spun up, and the craft rose off the ground. He depressed the accelerator, and the rover-sled was moving even before the containment seal was made.

Casmir popped his facemask open. Deidra did the same.

"Kick the communications system on, Deidra," he said. "Make sure the guidance coordinates are proper."

"We're on course." she said as she pressed icons and scanned the resulting images. "What was that?"

High-velocity piloting had been fun when he was younger. Now it was just one big butt clench. The antigrav drive kept the rover-sled off the ground without much input in most cases, but its response was sluggish. To go fast, the pilot had to guide everything. Casmir avoided a rising cliff and skimmed past a patch of sharp rock. A hard wind blew him off to his right, and the sound of the engines moaned behind them. After a moment he relaxed his grip and settled into a more stable frame of mind.

"That was a UG patrol," he said. "I was stupid enough to be paying attention only to the place I was looking."

"What did they want?"

He shrugged. "Who knows?"

"Are they okay?"

"They'll be fine."

"Really?"

"Yes, really. They'll be fine."

Only then did Deidra relax.

He reached over and rubbed the top of her head. She ducked and shied away.

"Stop it."

He smiled and steered around a boulder. His knees began to hurt again, and breathing felt like sucking swamp water. He gave a phlegmy cough. He wondered what the UG patrol wanted, too. Their aggression in this case surprised him, and sticking around to find out what they wanted was a risk he wasn't willing to take with Deidra.

He glanced to his dataskin.

The use of the network attack would tell the UG that he was there, which meant that more patrols would be coming soon. That was how it was for him. The fight never ended, and vigilance could never be relaxed.

Seeing Deidra absorb the story had been worth it, though.

Seeing the look on her face now as the impact of the UG's attack settled over her just made it better.

She already wanted to be like Perigee.

This attack would do nothing but speed that along.

"How about you call your mother," he said. "She'll be worried."

"I'm fine."

He smiled.

"Then how about you call in to the controller with our status? Tell them we left four sleepers, and to heighten all security measures."

"All right," she said with a smile.

"And when you're done with that, tell them to let your mother know you are all right."

CHAPTER 6

The Hive: Mars
Local Solar Date: February 12, 2206
Local Solar Time: 1005 Hours

Deidra waited by the access door. "Come on, Papa," she said.

The air lock was a smooth, bulbous outcropping that rose from the ground like a ramp and gave access to a convex hatch. The door engaged as he approached, its steel rim gleaming in the sun as the portal swung open. A ring of heated gas came as a cloud of vapor as it met the atmosphere.

Once the door was sealed and the atmosphere swapped out, they sat on the composite bench and doffed their surface suits.

Casmir sat upright to ease pressure from the small of his back.

The air was cool and fresh, but breathing deeply gave him another chest-rattling cough that pained his ribs.

"Brilliant," Deidra said as she dropped her gloves to the floor. Her dark hair was pasted against the side of her face.

"Don't pretend you're not going to clean those," he said, pointing to the gloves.

"The service will get them," she replied.

"We clean our own suits," Casmir said, raising his eyebrows.

Deidra wasn't wrong. The system techs could, in fact, come along behind them and clean their suits. But his CF meant a simple cold could knock him sideways, and an infection could literally kill him. He could still hear his mother's voice as she drilled into him the idea that cleaning his own pressure suit was something he would always do. *Don't blame anyone else if you don't clean it yourself.* He had been doing it for so long now that the process had become almost a ritual.

She bent to pick them up.

"Do a good job," he said.

Casmir worked bactericide over every piece of his own equipment as he removed it, kneading the cleaner into creases at the elbows and knees, and pulling the fingers of each glove inside out to expose those surfaces.

When he was finished, Casmir folded the suit, placed it into its cubby, then wrung his hands to get his circulation going again.

Deidra was still working, so he stretched his muscles and grabbed a towel to dry his hair. Wet hair made the lungs produce more mucus, and more mucus was the last thing he needed now. The movement helped too, because raising his arms made him feel better, though it brought on another tickle in his chest and caused a spear of pain to tweak his spine.

Deidra raised up to stow her suit and helmet in the right place.

She was like her mother—tall for her age.

Her arms were as thin as a dancer's, and her fingers long and graceful. Her coarse hair was damp with sweat, which made it curl up in those tight clumps she despised. She wore a sleeveless top under her suit, also darkened with sweat at the base of her perfectly formed back.

Through the observation window, Yvonne was now waiting for them.

He waved and stood up.

She smiled back, standing patiently in her kimono.

Yvonne was nearly as thin as when they first met, though her hair was going gray and her crow's feet had deepened. It bothered him that she worried so much now. He was a grown-up. He could take care of himself. That said, she was the most capable person he knew, and she didn't get that way by not worrying about things.

He cleared his throat again and realized that Matt Anderson and a detail of three guards were also standing beside Yvonne.

Anderson, at twenty years old, was bright and dedicated. He was the son of Gregor Anderson, Casmir's closest aide, and already more ambitious than his father ever had been. Unlike Yvonne, Matt was dressed, as always, in more formal attire—a pair of dark pants and a light blue jump jacket creased at the shoulders. A crisp Universe Three patch of red and yellow blazed from the left shoulder.

The stern expression on Matt's face returned Casmir's attention to the urgency of the moment. He noticed the set of his wife's jaw, and the sharp tone of her eyes. The guards behind them were also tense, standing as if truly on guard rather than just working on a detail.

Suddenly everything tasted metallic.

"Hurry," he said to Deidra. "You don't want to be late to your own party."

Casmir pressed the toggle, and the redundant pressure-locks let them through the gate. He stepped into the control center, his booted feet feeling almost too firm against the rubber floorplates.

The guards stood without speaking. Two techs sat behind control stations, one monitoring the air lock, the other controlling the ventilation system. All of them seemed to stand so awkwardly that even Deidra seemed to feel the tightness of the room.

"What's happened?" Casmir said.

"Have you taken a C-Pak?" Yvonne replied as she handed him a Byzantine cube. It was a cipher block, a mechanism to ensure eyes-only messages were properly received.

He dismissed her medical question with a wave of his hand, looking instead at the data block.

Black text glowed on a silver screen.

The first few lines contained encryption sequences, then came a fractal marker that had been set by the originator—a countermeasure that would destroy both the message and the host machine if something other than the proper Byzantine reader managed to get hold of it.

The message read: *The orange fox has jumped.*

He looked at Yvonne. The tingle of a cough rose in his throat. The UG patrol suddenly made sense.

"When?" he said, forcing the cough down.

"Less than an hour ago."

He scanned the date and time. The message had arrived at the Hive just eight minutes ago, meaning their mole had turned the information around in nearly real time.

"I'll be damned," he said.

"What's happening, Papa?" Deidra said.

Matt Anderson replied. "The United Government has just created a wormhole energy source in Alpha Centauri A that they will use to power their Excelsior class spaceships."

"The Star Drive?" Deidra's face clouded. "That means they can travel anywhere in the galaxy they want to go?"

"Yes," Casmir said. "That is exactly what it means."

"Can *we* do that?"

He glanced at his daughter.

His staff had been aware of the *Everguard* mission since well before it launched. They had planned for this moment for years, but the first thing that struck Casmir's mind right then was how quickly Deidra had processed this news and how quickly she had moved from understanding the nature of the threat to comparing the strengths and weaknesses of their groups.

Already she was thinking like a leader.

"Can we, Papa?" she asked again. "Can we travel faster than light?"

"Don't worry about that for now," he replied, putting his hand on her shoulder. Fierce or not, working on how Universe Three would respond to the UG's act of aggression was not something a thirteen-year-old should be dealing with. "Today it is your birthday. You have parties to attend."

"But I *want* to worry about it now."

"Later," he said, clearing his throat again and glancing at Yvonne for support.

"Take a C-Pak," Yvonne said as she led Deidra away. "Now."

What she really meant was that he needed to go see Dr. Iwal, but she wasn't going to chastise him that far in front of the rest of the room.

Casmir waited until they were gone, then turned to Matt Anderson.

"Tell your father we will meet to discuss our response this afternoon—" He glanced at a clock. "—at 1430."

"Yes, sir."

As the young man left, Casmir coughed and reached into his pocket for a C-Pak.

It was a thin film filled with a concoction of designer antibiotics, antihistamines, and other anti-inflammatory meds that could keep him running for a bit. The microscopic ridges of the patch affixed itself to his skin as he slapped it onto his forearm. A minute later, his body had absorbed it and he was breathing better.

He held his walking stick at his side as he stepped out of the room.

He had a brief to listen to now, a birthday party to attend, and then a meeting to lead.

Dr. Iwal would have to wait.

CHAPTER 7

The Hive: Mars
Local Solar Date: February 12, 2206
Local Solar Time: 1505 Hours

"So it's settled," Gregor Anderson said. "Operation Starburst will launch immediately."

Heads nodded, but Gregor was second in command, so his word wasn't enough. The twelve-member leadership team focused on Casmir.

The room they were in was large for a room in the Hive, oblong, with nearly ten meters to the longest dimension. Despite the air-handling system working overtime, the air here was clammy and warm.

Universe Three's leadership team had taken the last half hour to review three preplanned responses to news that the UG Star Drive mission had been successful.

The first, Operation Lift, was a tricky play, meant to destroy the Star Drive spacecraft.

The Houdini Maneuver was a mass kidnapping plan that Casmir thought had little chance of success even when it had been devised.

And finally, Operation Starburst was a more audacious maneuver, but one that would definitively change the game: a hijacking gambit that would provide U3 a true advantage as well as make the grandest of statements a group like theirs could make.

Operation Starburst directly targeted the UG's PR-driven Starburst event planned as the first major mission in UG's portfolio—a grandiose exercise that would send all four of their new Excelsior class Star Drive spacecraft on concurrent jaunts to four different star systems. To disrupt that mission would be akin to putting a knife through the ribs of the UG command structure. Operation Starburst's success would go straight to the competency of the United Government as a whole. It would also expose Universe Three as a direct threat.

Casmir flexed his fingers and drew a clean breath, taking an instant to dwell on his sense of free movement. The C-Pak had done wonders.

As he cleared his throat, the door to the chamber swung open and Tamira Weston, a young member of the communications center, stepped into the chamber. She let the door shut behind her, then waited until the room quieted.

"What is it, Tamira?" Casmir said.

Weston hesitated, her gaze flickering to Casmir and then away.

"Perhaps the director would like to hear this alone," she said.

"Please feel free to speak openly," he replied. "Any news we have now has to be freely available to everyone here."

"Europa is reporting they've been attacked, sir," Weston said.

It was as if the entire room did a double take.

Deego Larsi, the group's logistical planner, gasped.

"Attacked?" Casmir said.

"Their communication station reports three explosions, almost certainly bombs on a sequence wire. They say their containment seals are damaged."

The younger Anderson stood so sharply that the chair behind him slid away. Anger reddened his cheeks, and his shoulders and biceps bulged under his skintight shirt as he leaned his clenched fists against the table. "I can't believe the bastards would do something like this."

Voices rose.

Gregor Anderson grabbed his son's arm and pulled him downward as if to get him to take a seat despite the lack of his chair. The young man shook his father off, but went to retrieve the chair. Through the tangle of sound, Casmir heard Kazima Yamada, his chief engineering adviser, whispering to herself:

sonofabitch…sonofabitch…sonofabitch.

As was Casmir's preferred approach, Universe Three had set up camp on Europa nearly two decades ago, several standard years before the United Government had tried to annex the place—with their normal chest-beating pomposity, of course, as if annexation was the highest achievement a tiny block of ice in Jupiter's realm could possibly aspire to. His goal was to always be a step ahead of the UG—to arrive at a strategic location early enough to establish a self-sustaining culture that would resist the raw power of the United Government's capitalistic barbarism.

His teams had done good work.

They staked out the ice fields that Europan kelpiefish used as their breeding grounds, an act that served to restrict UG stooges from overharvesting the creatures in their first few years on the satellite. Admittedly, Casmir didn't care as much about the kelpiefish as he did about keeping the UG from making political headway, but if nothing else the species was a scoreboard, a way to judge progress. If the kelpiefish were here, U3 was winning; if they were gone, UG imperialism would rule. And, of course, while a kelpiefish was no silver bow, it was a form of life. The idea that they hadn't lost population of the species when masses of humans arrived on Europa made him feel like they had accomplished *something.*

In those early days Universe Three had also planted discontent among the population of Europa's private hydrogen miners, many of whom had toiled on the floes for long years before Universe Three's people arrived. Those earliest colonists were already wildcatters, so it hadn't been hard to inject them with solidarity against the UG.

And it had worked.

Europa was a clean system now, one of the few segments of the Solar System that could be developed without the UG's oversight. The U3 station on Europa was important for that reason alone, but it was just as important to Casmir because its mere existence had been Perigee's idea to begin with. She had concocted the plan late one evening over cocktails at one of the earliest parties wherein the concept that would eventually become Universe Three was hatched.

The voices of his leadership team jumbled together until he

raised one thin hand.

"How many dead?" he asked Weston when the sound had calmed.

"Three people, sir. No report on wounded."

"That's outrageous," Gregor Anderson said. "We've got to do something."

"Attack fire with fire, I say," replied Yamada, who spoke often about those early teams on Europa. "We can't leave this alone." Yamada was an engineer by degree, but a political strategist by vehemence. She had deep skin in the game and was clearing reeling.

"What do you think, Gregor?" Casmir said, already knowing what his friend would say.

The elder Anderson gave the dramatic nasal-toned inhale that Casmir had expected. Lines creased the corners of his lips, and his coffee-brown eyes darkened as he put his hands in his lap and looked back at Casmir.

"It's a diversion," he said.

"Please say more."

"We're fools if we think the UG is stupid. They know we've got something up our sleeves to respond to the wormhole, and they want us to be too busy saving our asses to take any action that might sabotage the Starburst program."

Yamada spoke. "It wouldn't be the first time they've done something like that."

"That's right," Casmir replied. "The fact is, I've always admired UG's intelligence people. They've consistently built highly effective operations that the average slob behind a news slate would never see as anything more than a simple squabble among riffraff on the fringe."

"Who, of course," Gregor added, "none of those average slobs actually care about."

"Exactly," Casmir said.

A sense of momentum built that told Casmir it was time to step up.

He glanced at Tamira Weston, who was the essence of his team's anxiety as she stood before the closed door. No matter how much she promised to keep quiet, Weston would eventually tell people about this moment. The words he chose now would make a difference in more ways than one.

He stood, thanking the powers that he had doubled the C-Pak just before the session, and ran his hand deliberately through his hair.

"It is true that I often admire UG strategists, but the fact is that the actions they take are illegal as hell. And it is also true that they get away with them because they understand that the public could care less about the methods they use to bring 'peace' to places like Europa—as long as that same public doesn't have to actually digest their methods. It's a truth as old as humanity that, while a few heads may get knocked around out in the wilds, that was to be expected."

He paused.

"This action of theirs on Europa is no different in the end. And as Gregor suggests, I am certain it's a diversionary tactic—an attack to draw our focus from the real issue at hand, which, of course, is the existence of the life-changing technology that allows for faster-than-light travel."

Some in the team nodded, but none spoke.

"But this exercise proves to me beyond any doubt that they don't understand who we are."

He looked at Yamada. "You see that, don't you?"

Yamada pursed her lips. "Their action assumes we are merely responsive."

Casmir looked at young Tamira Weston.

"Do you understand?"

"No, sir."

He was impressed the youth spoke firmly at that moment.

Perhaps she didn't understand the true nature of just how important this moment was, specifically with regards to Universe Three but quite possibly all of humanity.

"Their action," Casmir replied in an educational tone, "assumes that we have nothing already in place. It tells me they are unaware that we've been thinking about this for years, that they are unaware of the people we have already established in hundreds of places around the Solar System."

The set of her lips told him she understood.

"So it tells me—reminds me, actually—that they are incapable of looking beyond their own noses. It says to me that they have no idea what we are capable of. In the end, it tells me we will win."

He took in the rest as he paused.

"It is unfortunate that this time has come," he said. "But given the situation before us, I agree that Operation Starburst is the only proper response to the UG's Star Drive program."

"What about Europa?" Matt Anderson said. "We can't leave our people stranded there. If these UG actions have damaged their atmospheric controls, they'll have ripped up its radiation cover, too. Without those, Jupiter's emissions will fry them real soon now."

Casmir looked at the elder Anderson, then at Yamada, then back to the younger Anderson, who was slowly gaining control of himself.

"I will need anyone not involved in Operation Starburst to work with Ms. Weston here to find out what Europa needs, and get it to them. Beyond that, we'll need an extraction team. I want it on its way tonight."

"It's too tight, Casmir," Eugene Rickell, the team's supply leader, said. "Tomorrow is the best we—"

He cut the man off with a scythe-like wave of his hand.

"Just the idea of Universe Three leaving Europa sets my teeth on fire," he said. "But the fact is that whatever happens now will change our relationship with the United Government forever. Our people are no longer safe. So Matt is right. We need to be there for them if we ever want them to be here for us. You will work with Deego and anyone else you need to make this happen."

"Let me call Io Station," Deego Larsi broke in. "They are nearby, and should have spare equipment. That would reduce the immediate problem, but I'll have to get them something in return."

"Whatever they want," Gregor Anderson said. "Make it happen."

"All right."

The room dropped to total silence.

"The rescue and extraction operation will launch at 2100 hours tonight," Casmir said. "Earlier if possible."

He glanced around the room before his gaze fell back to Rickell.

The two of them had been through a lot together, and Casmir understood exactly how much pressure he was putting onto the man, especially in front of the rest of the team.

"Any questions?" Casmir asked.

"I understand," Rickell replied.

"No, sir," Yamada, aggressive as always, added. "No questions."

Casmir scanned his team.

A feeling of velocity filled the moment, an invisible but deadly sense of purpose that radiated from each of them like particle fields off a black hole. Even Casmir was surprised to feel more energized. That was the thing about clarity. Clarity begets certainty, and certainty allows for movement.

"Leave it to UG to make Operation Starburst seem like the easy job," he said.

The team's chuckle was nervous, but it was a chuckle.

"All right, then," Casmir said. "We're now Go for Launch. Let's all get to work."

The Art of Waiting

CHAPTER 8

Kensington Station, Asteroid Belt: Section 912
Local Solar Date: February 13, 2206
Local Solar Time: 1206 Hours

Kensington Station was a piece of junk.

Katriana Martinez, a security systems officer, second class, for the Excelsior project, sat at an empty booth in the station's dimly lit cafeteria and laid her rubber-rimmed datapad beside the plastic plate that held something the ship's processing system called a three-egg frittata, complete with bean paste and cheese. She had been stationed here for a year, about nine months longer than it took to decide she hated it.

At first, Katriana thought being stationed here would be no different from going to school, a gig she did for six years, and one that also took her away from people she loved, setting her down alone and silently afraid in a distant place where she mostly stayed in her assigned space and minded her own business. But Kensington was a cranky old station that something around thirty-five thousand people called home. It came complete with creaks and groans and exposed metal bulkheads, and was filled with the smell of molding machine oil. For her it was like a jail cell. It was a self-contained biosphere stuck in the isolated wildlands of the asteroid belt that felt different from anywhere else she had ever been. Despite the thousands of people who made up the staff, it felt obscenely vacant at its core, like one of those dilapidated mansions on the islands where folks who were mostly out of work took root, the places everyone used to say were haunted.

And it was cold.

She pulled her jacket tighter, but it didn't come close to combating her chill. Katriana found herself shivering even though the compartments were kept at a standard 22.5 degrees C.

The place was built as a halfway house where UG solar ship crews could refuel and get a brief respite from travel. It was also a remote research shop for UG engineers to practice their secret wizardry away from prying eyes. As all such transfer centers become, the station was also a hub for black market commerce and off-line information transfer: aka, scuttlebutt. Not that Katriana cared much about that. She was more focused on the fact that Kensington was the central hub for all logistics associated with the construction of Excelsior class spacecraft, which, of course, were soon going to be famous for their Star Drives.

That was the plan, anyway.

Today, however, as she sat down to gnaw her lunch, she was just tired: tired of twelve-hour work shifts, tired of Pisha Kalliente and her incessant jabbering, tired of waiting.

The cafeteria's floor was a synthetic material laid over the artificial gravity system. The walls were tiled with a mosaic of yellow and white. A dome that had probably once been sky-blue rose above the pavilion, threatening to crash down upon them like a frozen tidal wave. The configuration made for a perfect echo chamber, merging the sound of hundreds of voices into a single jumble that was as mushy as her three-egg plate of goo.

She was tired of that, too.

The artificialness of the entire place made Katriana sick.

She ran her hand through her golden hair and forked a bite of the frittata. It was too cold at the center, and too chewy at the edges. She sipped coffee that did nothing but make her stomach twist up in knots.

So much for the idea that the frittata would be a substitute for home.

That had been crazy thinking from the beginning. As if a bland glop of reheated protein paste could ever take the place of the frittatas she made herself, or her mother's pork *empanadillas*, spiced up with fresh guava and cracked pepper. A warm place grew in her chest at the memory of her father standing over a steaming pot of *asopao*, spooning the stew and breathing in big lungfuls of the peppery essence of garlic and onions that would fill the room.

The poor little frittata never stood a chance.

She picked at the datapad. Her in-box registered twenty-eight messages. As she worked through them, a shadow darkened the table.

"Mind if I join you?"

Orlando Jackson, an electronics tech, stood beside the small booth with a steaming bowl of chili on the tray in his hand.

"I would rather be alone, if that's all right," she replied.

"Oh, uh, sure," the tech said. "All right."

She watched from the corner of her eye as Jackson ambled to a table full of men. Their laughter hit her like a cold blast.

Assholes.

She was tired of them, too.

Did they think she didn't know what they said about her? Did they think she hadn't heard them call her everything from the classic "Station Bitch" to the much more original "232," a backhanded reference to the first robot that had explored the frigid surface of Pluto—and now was presumably embedded in a creeping block of the planetoid's dry ice?

For the ten thousandth time she thought about coloring her hair.

Nothing brought attention like a thin woman with a golden mane, but it was her own goddamned hair. She shouldn't have to hide it just because testosterone-laden space jockeys couldn't keep their pants on.

The men laughed again. Jackson had probably just lost a bet.

She hoped it was at least a week's pay.

Focus, Katriana, she thought. *Focus.*

The muscles around her eyes tightened as she concentrated on the datapad. She hated the people here. She despised the whole concept behind the Star Drive project—trillions of solar dollars thrown into a mission whose goal was merely to steal resources from another system.

It was obscene.

She thought of her little girls, Rosa and Talia, buried now in the dirt of San Juan.

Their bodies may well have returned to the land, but their spirits remained attached to every atom in her body, stuck inside her anger like one of those ancient insects buried in amber. That anger, the flare of pain that came when she let herself think of them, made her feel ugly, but it was better to feel ugly than to let them fade.

Through her periphery, she took in Orlando Jackson and his buddies, still laughing.

They wouldn't be so jovial if they knew what she was here for.

They wouldn't laugh if they understood that Security Systems Officer Katriana Martinez was also an opertative with Universe Three. They wouldn't crack jokes if they knew she graduated from an underground training program in Puerto Rico well before coming to Solar Command, and they wouldn't laugh if they knew there were a hundred other sleepers just like her stationed on Kensington. Her identity as a deep agent was the only thing that made the rest of this back-assed assignment bearable.

Her stomach churned as she picked at her lunch. The chatter from the men's table burned in her.

Patience, she thought. *Patience.*

Katriana Martinez was a secondary officer on Kensington's stationwide security team, but due to changes in UG security policy she had been cross-trained as a navigation specialist—a process that allowed the UG intelligence and security offices to keep their hands in the game in the early stages of any project. Assuming the *Everguard* mission completed on schedule, she was due to be billeted on *Icarus* as navigation specialist until the organization was certain the ship was secure, then she would be assigned back into a more traditional role: chief computer security officer.

Over the past two weeks, Lieutenant Commander Wagner, her UG CO, had doubled the intensity of the team's exercises, a step that meant twice daily runs on each Star Drive spacecraft in addition to their normal monitoring and law enforcement roles. Staff officers had been disappearing for days at a time. Communication from Command had gone suddenly silent.

All these were signs that something was up, and since it was possible *Everguard* could finish its mission any time, it didn't take Katriana any great mental acrobatics to guess what that something might be.

She chewed processed cheese, then cleared her throat.

"Can I see my messages, Abke?"

Abke, the station's self-contained Autonomic Bioprocessing Knowledge Engine, sent a list to her datapad that was sorted by priorities she had set earlier.

Roster assignments from Wagner were on top, followed by a commandwide policy change with regard to liberty—as if that mattered. Other internal discussion chains were next.

Then she saw something from her mother.

Adrenaline washed over her. It took all her self-control to keep from jumping straight to that message. She didn't break training, though. She hung tight. Business first. That was her way. To break the process now would be a small thing, but it would be a thing and Katriana knew exactly what kind of tracking and analysis mechanisms UG security teams had in place. If something was actually up, those systems would be on high alert.

So she read everything in its proper order.

The clamor of the cafeteria folded into the background as she responded to a question about a cipher key, then worked through an inane issue that had resulted in the station's dual password protocol locking down a private data core. She tagged a few notes onto the archive for use in later troubleshooting before finally getting to her mother's note.

It was chitchatty.

Her father was doing well, still gardening. Her mother was worried that he wasn't going to go to his normal checkup. One brother was in school, the other had taken a junior partnership in a law firm specializing in Earth/Martian trade law.

It was all false, of course.

Katriana's father farmed a plot of land in Puerto Rico. Her mother had passed years ago of complications arising from pesticide poisoning that the cane farmers had lobbied to put into place to ensure their profits didn't drop.

The note's closing sent a chill down her back.

Nos vemos en las estrellas.

See you in the stars.

Her hand shook as she sipped her coffee.

The men in Orlando Jackson's group laughed and joked again,

but this time she grinned like she might be the Cheshire cat.

It was started.

The public-address system crackled.

"Ladies and gentlemen of Kensington Station," the voice came over the stationwide channel. "This is Admiral Gleason speaking. I have exciting news from the *Everguard* mission."

Chapter 9

Kensington Station, Asteroid Belt: Section 912
Local Solar Date: February 15, 2206
Local Solar Time: 0800 Hours

Two days later *Sunchaser*, the first of the UG's four Excelsior class vessels, attached itself to the feed from Alpha Centauri A, lit its Star Drive engine, and made its maiden trip to Barnard's Star and back in less than a day.

The crew did not suffer the aging effects of Einstein's famous twins. Traveling at speeds faster than light had not sent anyone ahead in time, nor, as a few mathematicians had continued to predict, did it send anyone backwards.

As famed Princeton professor and now Nobel laureate Ranya Denaldi quipped in summing up her Theory of Space and Time, "Photons move in accordance with the laws of relativity, but time is its own master." *Sunchaser*'s confirmation of her theory made Denaldi an instant icon, and her v-book, which was half dissertation and half memoir, became an overnight bestseller. In the aftermath of the *Sunchaser*'s maiden voyage other mathematicians and astrophysicists took turns toasting themselves and speaking with hyperbolic excitement on news shows and discussion bands.

For the layman, interviews of crew members were just as

fascinating.

"It was like stepping into a tunnel of neon," one crew member said.

A rash of holo games were released a day after the news, setting off a spending spree greater than any recorded before.

In the hallways of aerospace companies throughout the Solar System, however, a different fervor took shape.

Sunchaser's second mission would be to retrieve *Everguard*'s triumphant admiral. Then would come Starburst—the UG's ostentatious show of force that would simultaneously send all four Excelsior class Star Drive vessels on their way, each with separate mission profiles that would begin the story of humanity's entry into intergalactic exploration.

After those gaudy missions, talk would turn to colonies and exploration.

Targets were already being generated. Young families were already considering career options in services and systems that might well support new cities on distant planets.

For Katriana Martinez, however, things were a bit more straightforward. The next few days were a blur of security checks, priority reviews, and system diagnostics. She moved from one session to the next, barely eating and sleeping even less.

Lieutenant Commander Wagner had a lot riding on this program—as they all did, she supposed. He pushed his crew hard.

"Sleep is for those who can afford to fail," he said at a team meeting late one night, ignoring two centuries of behavioral science that suggested otherwise.

This wasn't a problem for Katriana, though. She wanted to work through it all because whenever she felt tired or drained, and would then close her eyes in the quiet of any moment that presented itself, she found the faces of her girls staring back at her. She felt their presence with her. She felt them intertwined in her thoughts. And when it wasn't Rosa and Talia, it was one of the others. In a silent nook on the second day she found herself thinking of her daughters' father, who had been conscripted to the army the week they were born and who she had not seen since.

This kept her focused on her job.

While everyone else was buzzing about how the idea of visiting the farthest reaches of the galaxy had just moved from the realm of physics to the domains of engineers, Katriana kept her mind on the tasks of making her way through the exercises before her.

Operation Starburst was near.

For her, the fun was still to come.

Operation Starburst

NEWS

SOURCE: INFOWAVE — NEWS for the twenty-third century
TRANS: UGIS SUNCHASER
TRANS DATE: March 12, 2206, Earth Standard
HEADLINE: Operation Starburst Prepares to Blast Off!

*Starburst, the first multiple-craft Star Drive mission, is a marketer's dream. With a churning mass of fused hydrogen and helium from the Alpha Centauri A wormhole pipeline ready to fuel their power plants, four Excelsior spacecraft—*Sunchaser, Einstein, Orion, *and* Icarus—*are now due to light their engines at the same time.*

If this sensational launch sequence is successful, the crews of each spacecraft will experience faster-than-light travel as the four ships are launched in four different directions in an event that some have called a modern-day ode to Buck Rogers and Han Solo. They will explore faraway worlds and return in less than two days' time, each bringing home more raw data about remote star systems than has been collected in the millennia before.

"It's like a weekend jaunt," Fleet Admiral Jenniah Gleason said yesterday. "But, of course, in this case it's a working weekend."

Chapter 10

Kensington Station, Asteroid Belt: Section 912
Local Solar Date: March 12, 2206
Local Solar Time: 2357 Hours

Knowing she wasn't going to get much rest anyway, Katriana settled into her sleeper after an eighteen-hour shift. The cell was a small fold in the security systems block—her own little slice of heaven a meter wide and another meter tall, just deep enough for her to stretch out comfortably. She had painted one side pink, the other a mishmash rainbow of colors that reminded her of a finger painting Rosa had done once. The ceiling was an active array that piped in video and other system information from the command structure.

If she were ever to have been bumped a rank, perhaps she would have gotten a unit big enough to hold a holo projector, or if she were ever to declare as a pairing with a shipmate, she could get a bigger sleeper, too, but neither of those were going to happen.

That was fine, though.

She was happy enough with her enclosed walls and her hand-painting. The cramped space was good because it reminded her of her girls, and that's what mattered most.

Forgetting was not an option.

A cool breeze of air filtered through the sleeper and raised goosebumps on her arms. She lay still and let her muscles melt into the mat. An endless loop of numbers flashed through her head—code sequences that she had been working with all day, execution orders and decision tree checkoffs that were part of Wagner's drills.

She thought about taking a tab of drite to help her sleep, and maybe plugging into Abke for a holo that would mold her dreams.

Instead, she asked for her mail.

Which is where she found a message from her brother, Carlos.

The memo was full of triviality and a suggestion that she should clear time to get together for a summer vacation. It was a code, of course. The file containing the message carried an executable program inside its tight, triple-layered wrapper. As her eyes scanned the phrase *Nos vemos en las estrellas,* the input routine on her reader scanned her retinal signature, and the code block released itself.

So much for sleep tonight.

The knowledge of what was about to happen made her heart race.

Despite the fact that Interstellar Command probably couldn't stop them now even if they were scanning the data logs and looking for anomalies, she decided to match her established behavioral pattern and read the message a second time. It probably wasn't necessary, but the process of reading twice was ingrained inside her and it made her feel better to follow the ritual of protocol all the way to the end, so she read it a second time, surprised to find it actually seemed to help her stomach. Regimentation was apparently her friend.

"Abke," she said. "Please close memo Carlos Martinez twelve."

As the message closed, code ran across her processor: Photons raced through optical tracing and quantum transistors to channel logic inside her system that connected up with the shipboard security systems. The software peeled back the base communication protocol that ran Kensington Station's core operations, then, as it dug deeper, stripped the multiple layers of encryption that the UG used to guard against internal corruption. All messages that arrived at Kensington Station carried these two layers. But the code from the Carlos memo accessed a third, transparent protocol, a randomly switching interface that required additional manipulation from Katriana's master key.

She gave the reference, and rather than porting the return message to her screen, this third interface sent the data embedded in Carlos's memo down a different path.

The mail closed after the program finished executing.

The file, an activation profile, was now waiting for her, encased in a shell on her home memory space and filled with a set of coordinates that pointed to a sector in space that she wasn't privy to.

Next she had to break into each craft's unique control systems.

Each Excelsior spacecraft had its own set of security walls—one for propulsion, another for the bridge, food services, navigation, and so on. Each craft also had a unique master that overrode the rest on that craft. Finally, an overlord pattern also existed—a multidimensional, fractal-encoded skeleton key that opened all systems in all spacecraft. The overlord pattern was primarily used to provide for common upgrades and system troubleshooting of every ship in the dock at any one time, and it was controlled by someone higher than even Wagner.

The Carlos program created a key that fit Interstellar Command's overlord pattern.

Katriana didn't know how Universe Three had obtained that key, nor did she care to know. The organization had been there for her when she needed them. They were reliable. Everyone did their jobs like the professionals Casmir Francis recruited them to be. This reliability was one of the things that told her she had made the right choice aligning with Universe Three. Pretty much anything a United Government coder did was guaranteed to need at least three passes of testing and remediation before it worked. Universe Three coders, on the other hand, had never failed her.

So it was no surprise that the interface came up as promised, and even less so that it worked the first time she ran it.

Not that it would have mattered in the end. Even if U3 software slingers had sucked, she would have stayed with them, but the fact that they were top-notch made her just that much more smug in her decision.

She opened the navigation controller and the security system, then she ran her activation profile.

The update code distributed changes.

Despite their own Intelligence Office's warnings, the United

Government had always acted like Universe Three was a simple fringe organization.

They were about to pay for their disregard.

CHAPTER 11

UGIS *Icarus*
Docked, Kensington Station, Asteroid Belt: Section 912
Local Solar Date: March 13, 2206
Local Solar Time: 0700 Hours

The following day, Katriana boarded Icarus exactly on schedule, went through the security stations, and took her position at the security systems monitor. Per protocol and as her commanding officer, Lieutenant Commander Wagner visited her for first-posting recognition.

"Congratulations on your assignment, Ms. Martinez," he said, standing before her. "I'm sure you'll be worthy of the honor." His hands were clasped behind his back, and he wore his work fatigues, which she supposed were intended to represent an industrial ethic on this historic day.

"Thank you, sir," she replied.

If she'd actually cared about the UG's assignment beyond her need to make it happen, just the idea she should feel *honored* for having been provided it would have served to hang her goat.

This was no *honor* she had been bestowed with.

It was a post she had *earned*. Her reward for three years of results, and months upon months spent focusing on nothing but her job. Specifically, she guessed it was for her work creating the surveillance code that had provided superiors with dirt on a group of insiders who were running law pods on the side: small factions of wildcatting executives who created areas of the Solar System that would operate essentially on their own, all while skimming back mounds of cash straight off the top for rigging up juicy supply contracts.

None of it mattered, though.

Her interest in UG politics was purely pragmatic.

If the uppers wanted to spy on their own people, she figured they would do it with or without her help and, law pods or not, they were all just UG folk who wanted the raw freedom to screw the people they wanted to screw. In the end, the only reason anyone cared about the podders was that their black markets made it hard for bigger companies to get their hooks into the asteroid mining zones.

But spying on the population was her front. Proof solid that she was UG to the bone, which was the Universe Three way. Rather than try to infiltrate higher levels to begin with, U3 started with a multitude of candidates in the lower ranks, and let the few who could rise, rise organically. Katriana's work modeled the processes perfectly. Put work above all things. Be quietly excellent, drive hard, and create an impeccable record.

Regardless, no, she would never feel *honored* to achieve a position.

Instead it should be her superior officers who felt *honored* she had driven herself to the point of a near physical breakdown so that they could continue to live the lives of such relative ease they were already living.

She saluted Lieutenant Commander Wagner, though, then sat at her station as he walked away. She dried her palms on the thighs of her red jumpsuit and waited for all the other rituals to finish.

The entire staff was here, forty-five officers and enlisted scattered around a large bridge that was shaped like a half circle. A huge observation screen dominated the forward panel of the ship, built into a curved section of the craft to give everyone in the room a direct view into open space. It was a view protected in-flight by a dynamic sensor shield designed to deflect microscopic objects in the same fashion that a magnetic field protects a planet from the solar winds. Rows and rows of numbers flashed a constant loop on the forward screen.

Behind her, Captain Boyer stood tall over the triple rows of command stations, looking stiff and worried despite the fact that all signals so far represented a perfect launch.

Katriana dried her hands one more time, embarrassed to be nervous after all her preparations.

Focusing on her girls only helped a little.

She wondered which of the other six hundred people it took to operate *Icarus* were U3 operatives. Of the forty-five on the bridge, she guessed at least three others were co-conspirators, but she wouldn't know who they were until the time came.

Pela Abedian, an E6 on the nav panel, looked jumpier than usual but she was a bit of a basket case anyway, so that could be standard preflight nerves. Engine Specialist Lenny Tash seemed more than a little distracted as he checked over Star Drive coolant parameters—but then Tash was always distracted.

Everyone was nervous today.

She focused on her station.

The upper corner of the screen showed the state of the real-time antivirus worm she had initiated earlier. It was working its way through the proper executables. The security system was registering green, just as it was supposed to.

Abke's voice came over the room. "Launch positions in five minutes."

She stared into the darkness of space.

Three hundred seconds had never felt so long.

Sunchaser's crew reported that FTL travel came with a light show better than the aurora borealis, and though she wanted to be all business, Katriana admitted she was interested to see that.

At the top of the bridge, Lieutenant Commander Wagner whispered into the captain's ear.

Katriana's heart rate spiked.

Could Wagner know something?

She glanced at her screen. It was still all green.

All morning she had been ultra-careful, going so far as to even avoid accessing her system to make sure she didn't screw up by accident. She kicked herself for that now—*not* accessing her system was an anomaly. Could the deviation have registered? Would the fact that she *hadn't* looked at her mail be the slip that gave her away?

She waited, but the captain did nothing but smile in response to Wagner's comments.

It had just been a joke—a one-liner or other such jovial aside between two friends.

She was okay.

At least, she was okay so long as she calmed down and didn't do anything stupid. She wiped her hands on her thighs again and took a breath, trying to remember the salted smell of the open ocean that surrounded her home Earthside.

"One minute to launch," Abke said.

The crew quieted. Status lights lit.

"Thirty seconds."

The petty officer in charge of launch coordination spoke loudly enough that his voice carried across the floor like a bullhorn. "We have green on the screen, Captain."

"Kick it on," Boyer replied.

"Aye, sir."

He entered his commands.

"Launch engines full thrust," Abke reported. "Multidimensional gate toggle set on timer. Five seconds…Four…Trim engines active…Two…One…and Go Launch."

The wormhole gate opened inside *Icarus*'s propulsion system.

Hydrogen and helium flowed through an extradimensional throat created by the folding of math onto physics; tendrils of energy fed back into the structure of the wormhole itself, thereby letting the device maintain its shape and provide for its own eventually cannibalistic existence. Fluid pressure rose in the compressor. Atoms rent and combined and scattered in billions upon billions of gluonic explosions.

Deep inside *Icarus*'s quantum computer, a software code toggled different switches than the project leaders had originally placed in the calibration.

A subroutine changed coordinates from one set to a newer one.

A series of functions accessed the newly modified data structure, and navigation parameters changed.

Control stations shut down their interfaces.

Weapon systems went off-line.

And finally…slowly…a toxic nerve gas that had been working

its way through the ship's air-handling system began to seep into the ship's command center.

Rivulets of color shimmered across the forward screen. Flashes of red, orange, and neon-metallic colors that Katriana hadn't believed could have existed a moment ago bloomed and flowed. A blue wave swirled, eventually twisting into a ghostlike dragon that flickered away into the ethereal beauty of the flight. Green lighting brought *oohs* and *aahs* from the crew. Energy billowed and pulsed. Stars became yellow flares.

Katriana did her best to keep her eyes on her screen as doors locked and systems ground to a stop.

Abedian was the first to notice a problem.

"I have an anomaly," she said loud enough to draw attention.

"Report," Captain Boyer replied with professional calm.

"Coordinates are incorrect, sir."

Another ensign running the Magnetic Sensor Board confirmed her report. "I have *Sunchaser* and *Orion* on the MSB, Captain," he said. "*Sunchaser* just over a million kilometers port at thirty degrees roll. *Orion* dead ahead at eight hundred thousand. I don't yet see *Einstein*. No…update that, sir. *Einstein* is within range also."

The pause was palpable.

Starburst was supposed to result in all Excelsior craft arriving at different star systems.

The central doorway snapped open.

Lieutenant Commander Timmon Keyes, a man responsible for the ship's environmental control team, held an energy weapon at his side. His face was drawn in deep lines, his eyes dark and sharp as he stepped forward. He was a big man, and his bearing said he was in control. He snapped a portable rebreather into place as he came farther into the command room.

Keyes, Katriana thought. That made sense.

The air-handling system itself was the operation's primary weapon delivery mechanism, and as environmental control, Keyes would be in charge of that portion of the operation.

"Let's all remain calm," Keyes said. "So no one gets hurt."

"What is this?" Captain Boyer said, stepping toward Keyes.

"Stay there," Keyes warned. "This will be over in a moment."

Boyer stopped.

"There's nothing wrong with the navigation parameters, is there, Ms. Martinez?" Keyes said.

All eyes turned to her.

"No," she replied. "There is nothing wrong."

Thoughts filled her head. Why weren't the people falling? Shouldn't she smell something by now? Would the vapor be odorless? Would the room temperature chill down, or was that just silliness? She had taken the antidote with breakfast, and wasn't sure if that changed her senses at all or not.

She put these questions aside as she looked at Keyes.

"We're in the Eta Cassiopeia system—exactly where I directed all four spacecraft to go."

With that, her fingers went to a pocket in her jumpsuit and extracted a small rebreather of her own—this she clamped between her teeth as she adjusted the fit around her head.

"I am taking command of *Icarus* in the name of Universe Three," Keyes said.

"This is a very big mistake, Lieutenant Commander," Boyer said, edging toward Keyes. He put his hand out, palm up. "If you give me your weapon, I'll do my best to see you're not discharged at the court-martial."

Keyes laughed. "Did you hear that, Ms. Martinez, Mr. Tash, and Ms. Nassir? He'll see that I'm not discharged!"

Engine Specialist Tash and Shipboard Weapons Commander Brooke Nassir both stood forward, withdrawing their own plasma guns and slipping on their rebreathers.

"Tempting, I'm sure," Tash replied.

Damn it, Katriana thought, *did I miss a direction? Should I have come armed, too?* No. She wouldn't have missed that. She was security, though, so her U3 controllers probably didn't want to risk her being found with an unregulated weapon on board. *That made sense*, she thought. And it made sense that others were protecting her.

"Oh, my God!" the ensign on the sensor station said.

"What is it?" the captain replied.

"I have an explosion at *Sunchaser*'s coordinates, sir." The ensign looked up. "She's gone."

"What do you mean?"

"They must not have followed their orders," Keyes said, a grin crawling over his lips.

The safety commander groaned, then fell over. While a crewmate bent to help him, another dropped.

A surge of joy rolled through Katriana.

This was it. The vapor had made it here. The game was over.

Nearly, anyway.

Now that *Sunchaser* had been destroyed and the cover on the operation was off, the rules changed. They had to keep the crew from taking control and returning the ship to the Solar System for as long as it took the vapor to do its thing.

"I'm sorry," Keyes said as he turned to the captain. "Another half minute and this would have been a lot easier."

Then he shot Boyer from point-blank range.

The captain hit the floor.

Silence hung in the air.

Then the bridge erupted.

Lieutenant Commander Wagner leapt at Keyes.

Keyes squeezed off a shot. The green energy hit Wagner in midflight, and he thudded onto the floor with a cry of pain and the smoldering smell of burnt flesh. Screaming voices echoed through the chamber. Keyes's weapon flared again and again. Tash and Nassir worked the other side of the room. A hand grabbed Katriana. She punched out to get away, then jumped on the back of a crewmate and yanked his head around by the chin until the neck snapped. The body slumped. She gritted her teeth and shoved it away, noticing it was Orlando Jackson.

Served the asshole right.

Served the whole damned station right—the whole damned Interstellar Command.

The UG had killed her girls, now she was returning the favor.

She stepped back to her command post. A man from the row below reached. She pivoted and kicked him away, and his body crashed with a thick *thwump* against the edge of the command station below.

The physicality of it all made her glad she didn't have a weapon, but it was over almost as fast as it began—the crew quickly falling to the vapor that was now fully deployed into the command center.

The four conspirators stood amid smoldering bodies and flashing control panels, breathing heavily. The taste of warm blood in Katriana's mouth told her she had bit her cheek, but she found she liked it. Its tang made everything clearer.

Keyes's eyes gleamed with passion.

"Secure all systems," he said. "Send the message that *Icarus* is now under U3 command."

"Aye, sir," she said.

Katriana closed her eyes for a brief moment as she turned to her command panel, and as she did she imagined the faces of two round-cheeked little girls in the darkness who laughed and played and smiled back at her.

Chapter 12

Chicago, Illinois
Local Solar Date: March 13, 2206
Local Solar Time: 1315 Hours

Willim June Pinot was a junior analyst in G-2, the counter espionage department within the United Government Intelligence Office. His primary assignment was to gather data, make assessments, and write reports about Universe Three and other subversive groups. It was interesting work, if a bit mind-numbing at times.

He had graduated from Yale a year prior with a political science major, a minor in journalism, and a second minor in Lunar studies.

Though his waist was already beginning to show the effects of a sedentary lifestyle, he was tall and naturally thin. His hair was dark and usually unkempt. This was because he was a man of his own keeping, and he had more important things to worry about than where every hair on his head might be at any particular moment.

He had turned twenty-eight years old exactly one week before.

For his birthday, the rest of the guys at G-2 took him out to Donahue's Pub, where they drank microbrew, watched the zero-g X-Factor games, and ate real French fries. It had been fun, a diversion from the usual process of going home, dropping a frozen tub into the micro, and playing Diplomacy on the net.

He was in his supervisor's office, Paul Kane, that day when a message came in under the red flash tag that meant Kane had to take it regardless of what else he was involved in.

"Kane here."

Pinot watched his boss's expression go from jovial, to concerned, to outraged in a matter of ten seconds.

"Are you serious?" Kane finally said. "Yes…I understand…I have one of the analysts in my office now. I'll call in the rest…Yes…Thanks, I'll call you back as soon as I know more."

The communication clicked off.

Pinot had never before seen his boss ruffled.

"What's wrong?"

"Have you seen anything that says Universe Three was mobilizing?"

"My last report discussed the evac operation on Europa," Pinot responded. His defensive shields were going up, and the analytical portion of his mind engaged.

Universe Three was a damned scary organization.

Casmir Francis was a charismatic, obstinate, and persistent leader, and unlike most leaders proposing radical changes he was willing to suspend his own chest-beating ethics and do whatever it took to get his way.

Pinot had written report after report about Francis, each of them noting that his superiors should expect trouble.

Of course, nothing had changed.

"Yes," Kane said. "I remember that. I was looking for something more."

"That report includes several sections," Pinot replied. "It suggests the organization had something in process, and tied them all to plans my earlier reports discussed might happen if we press them too far."

Kane made an expression that was half grimace, half smirk, and ran his hand down his coat lapels.

"What's happened?" Pinot said with the precise enunciation he took on whenever a problem began to coalesce in front of him.

"*Sunchaser* has been destroyed. Universe Three has control of *Icarus* and *Einstein*."

"*Orion?*"

"She's still ours. Universe Three is already publicly claiming responsibility."

Pinot let the news settle. "Holy shit," he finally said.

"I need everything you've got on U3," Kane said, "and I need it now. Resource reports, assumptions on special intel activity, recon, dark projects, legal activity, the latest status of their bases on Mars, Europa, and Io, and anything else you think has any bearing on the situation."

"I understand," Pinot replied. He would make it a point to include his status reports for the past six months in the package.

He looked at his boss and smelled the metaphorical scent of fresh meat.

Worry lines crossed Kane's face, and his skin seemed suddenly transparent.

Kane was going down. Pinot saw that. Somebody would hang for this, and his boss was almost certainly going to be the guy.

Kane drew a nasally breath.

"Go," he said. "We brief the CIO in two hours. I want you back here with a full story in forty-five minutes."

"I'll be ready."

"Thank you."

Chicago, Illinois
Local Solar Date: March 13, 2206
Local Solar Time: 1545 Hours

Sela Matz, Chief Intelligence Officer of the United Government, sat at a virtual table ringed with fifteen Intelligence executives, each physically located in their own niche of the sector and each with their own flock of analysts seated behind them. Her hair was coifed, and as crisply in place as the material of her dark business suit.

Data flashed on the table monitor, and maps and charts flickered as each member of the staff pored over millions of bytes of data, trying to make sense of the unthinkable. They had lost three Excelsior spacecraft, one killed, two hijacked. Tension was a nearly audible buzz throughout the room. The CIO needed to take a recommendation to the president in fifteen minutes.

Only Willim Pinot sat calmly, knowing it was too late to do anything now beyond taking in the activity and assessing the people in the organization as they reacted to the situation.

"What is your recommendation?" Matz asked, staring at Pinot's boss.

Kane straightened his collar.

"Universe Three is inflexible," he said. "They won't negotiate, as you can see from the fact that it's been several hours since the attack, and we haven't received anything from them beyond their publicly broadcast statement, which is nothing more than the basic 'no dissent, no freedom' rhetoric they always spout."

"That means?"

"That means we have to take care of this once and for all. No half-assed attempts to salvage relationships or ease anyone's minds. I recommend an all-out response. A total blitz. Focused on taking back the two spacecraft they took. We still have *Orion*, so I think we use her to track down *Icarus* and *Einstein*. At the same time, we press a full attack on every base and outpost they have. Pronto. Everything we've got. As soon as we can muster it. Make a statement and get rid of the problem in one massive step."

CIO Matz looked pointedly to Pinot. "Is that how you see it?"

The move surprised him, but really shouldn't have. Matz had actually read the same reports Kane hadn't.

He let the moment settle, then replied. "I—"

"Willim is behind me all the way," Kane said.

"The young man can speak for himself, Paul."

In that moment, Pinot pondered the situation.

Kane's proposal was dumb as shit. Universe Three was like a colony of cockroaches—they could scuttle for darkness with the best of them. Sure, a full-out attack would play well to the public and would let a few top government officials blow off some steam. It might even save a job or two. But it couldn't possibly solve anything.

It was, however, time for a bold response.

He and his boss had tussled over this, and up until now, of course, Kane had won. But it was clear to him that Kane was on the way out, and the Chief Intelligence Officer was asking Willim Pinot what he thought.

"U3 is so dangerous because they play the long game. And if you've been following my reports," he said, pausing pointedly for effect, "you'll see that while we've been able to keep them at bay, they've made gains in various key places every year. I agree with

Paul's view that we have to take an immediate action, but while I understand the optics of trying to regain *Icarus* and *Einstein* in such a public fashion, I worry about whether we can achieve that right now."

Kane pressed his lips together.

"Why?" Matz said.

"We don't know how to trace an Excelsior footprint, so until we figure out how to do that we won't find either *Icarus* or *Einstein* without quite a bit of luck. In addition, I've been following U3 for a long time. They didn't do this with a plan they drew up in the dirt."

"What are you saying?"

"I'm saying that when we get to their outposts, I suspect we'll find U3 operatives will either have bugged out, or be mostly defenseless private citizens who were simple dupes. We may want to take down every U3 outpost in the system for the message it sends to the public, but let's not pretend that it will make much of a difference in the end. And," he said, "I'm saying it takes a lot of energy to cover everything at once. I'm saying that might not be the best way to win against an opponent who's playing the long game."

Matz nodded.

"But," Pinot continued, "they do have three large, primary bases. We've already hit Europa with an operation that was designed to sap their strength. Taking out Io wouldn't be too hard, but there's not a lot of power in that step. The real key, I think, is Mars."

"Because Casmir Francis uses it as their headquarters?" Matz asked.

"Of course."

"So you're suggesting we focus on their Mars base?"

"Yes," Pinot said, noting Kane's grimace out of the corner of his eye. "I agree with Paul that we should strike, and strike fast. But if we're going to do maximum damage to the U3 organization, I say we focus everything we have on one place. Reduce their Mars colony to space slag as vengeance against the sabotage, and at the same time send a conciliatory broadcast on public channels that offers a complete cease fire in return for our ships back."

Matz tapped her fingertip on the tabletop, nodding in silent agreement as she considered the option.

"We'll have to hurry, though," Pinot said.

The tapping stopped, and Matz waited for him to continue.

"I have been following Casmir Francis for a very long time. He will have assumed we would counter something like this. He'll be prepping to bug out. I say we hit him with *Orion*, and with anything else we have, within the next twenty-four hours."

The corner of her mouth twitched upward.

"Anyone have anything to add?" she said.

She glanced at the clock embedded in the center of the table. When no one responded, the CIO dismissed the staff and walked briskly out to catch her ride to the president's office.

Pinot released a breath.

Kane scowled, but said nothing.

There was no doubt in anyone's mind whose advice the CIO was going to follow.

Bugout

CHAPTER 13

Mars: The Hive
Local Solar Date: March 14, 2206
Local Solar Time: 0445 Hours

Two ships! Casmir Francis thought, with a smile. *Two!*

He and Yvonne strode at a brisk pace down the Hive's main corridor, escorted by three guards. He was happy for the morning C-Pak regimen and a set of clear lungs as he leaned heavily on his walking stick. Voices called from everywhere around them. Loader bots rumbled up and down the automation lane. The ground crew scurried from bay to bay like they were under a perpetual code blue, which, effectively, they were. A bugout was a serious thing.

This was the last time he would ever see these hallways, but he was pathologically unable to keep down the excitement of the idea that Operation Starburst had succeeded beyond his wildest dreams.

Einstein and *Icarus* were theirs.

Sunchaser had been destroyed and *Orion* had escaped, but they had two Excelsior class spacecraft at their command.

The idea was staggering.

The UG wouldn't let this stand, though.

Universe Three had played cat and mouse with the UG for years, but you can't attack the fleet's Excelsior class spacecraft without drawing fire. Operation Starburst meant those days were gone, and it also meant that now much of the public would be behind the United Government. Despite the latest UG message that offered a truce for the return of the ships, Casmir knew the gloves were now officially off.

"I can't believe you got two ships," Yvonne said.

"Flattery will get you everywhere, my dear," he said, raising a lecherous eyebrow.

From an angle, Casmir caught the delightedly sly expression that crossed the face of the guard who was walking ahead of them. Two others followed behind. He wondered how they would tell the story of this conversation when they sat down to pubbing with their cohorts.

"This is it, though," he finally said. "No going back."

Yvonne pulled a tight smile. "It will all be fine. Just so long as we get out of here before the Uglies come."

He grinned at his partner's use of the derogatory term. It wasn't a word that often graced her lips, but apparently the idea that the UG might, at any moment, turn their home into a burnt-out trash heap had changed the game a bit for her, too.

"Are the kids ready?" he said.

"Already aboard."

"That's good."

Their footsteps echoed against a metal grate that lay over a broken segment of the corridor.

The last step in Operation Starburst was the immediate and complete evacuation of every major outpost they had, and given the public nature of the Hive and its proximity to other UG outposts, Mars had to happen fast. Timing was critical. Too early and U3 would tip their hand, too late and they would suffer the consequences. Already Casmir's spotters had reported surveillance drones and electronic scans picking up.

He expected direct UG advances within the hour.

"I'm worried about Io," he said, speaking his fears out loud. "They got a late jump."

"They've done their drills," Yvonne replied.

He smiled at her.

"What do you think, Ms. Barr?" he said to the lead guard. "Will Io be all right?"

The guard hesitated a moment, then spoke her mind.

"They can make up the time."

"That's what I needed to hear."

"It's the truth, sir," Barr said. "If it's true that they have been executing their drills as we have, Io will be fine."

They came to where the corridor opened to the final staging bay.

The hallway widened and a cool breeze blew over the back of Casmir's neck. Their already brisk pace quickened, adding a fresh sting to the chill. The smell of Martian dust was acrid here. Members of Universe Three gave him anxious glances as they made their way through the passage. He tried to maintain a sense of calm as they progressed, but the emotions of the moment welled in his throat and he had difficulty breathing. He gave a rumbling cough, which made Yvonne frown.

"You should have seen the doctor," she said.

"No time now."

"It takes only a minute."

He bit back a response because he knew she was right and because he knew that a lack of time wasn't really his problem.

His problem was that he could handle only one emergency at a time, and it annoyed him that she was worried about him. He was sick, but not an invalid. His last reading said his blood ox was fine enough, and his lung capacity reading was something over 90 percent. The C-Paks would serve him fine, even if he was now tripling up on them. Barring success of the UG response, he was going to live.

They turned a corner to find a woman sitting on a shuttle cart, clearly attempting to move a crate that had gotten wedged between three others. A man was held up behind them.

"Get out of the frickin' way!" the man said.

"Mind your own goddamned business, Bischoff. I'm not in your way."

"Shut up and get that crate out of here."

"Shove it, asshole."

"I know what I'll be shovin' if you don't hurry your ass up."

Casmir's guards moved to confront the pair, but Casmir raised his walking stick to stop them, and went forward instead. He strode toward the pair, came to a stop, and rested the staff against his thighs.

His voice boomed in the hallway. "I couldn't help noticing there seems to be a problem here."

The workers cringed when they realized who it was.

"Can anyone tell me what's wrong?"

"I'm sorry, sir," the man said. "She's in my way."

"I'm trying to get the computer core down to the primary shuttle," the woman answered before Casmir could ask. "It's got to be there now, but it's stuck."

"Yes," Casmir said. "We can't leave our systems behind."

The two stood silently.

"Tempers are high right now, eh? There is too much to do. Just remember, though, that you are on the same team and that on our team we will die only for those things we believe in."

"And we believe in the universe," the two replied in unison.

"Thank you." He pointed to the woman's cart. "If you would pull the end of your cart a bit further away from the wall, perhaps this gentleman would be able to get through."

"Yes, sir," the woman said.

Casmir turned to Bischoff. "And if you were to have slipped over closer to the wall, I think you could have made it through, anyway."

"I'm sure you're right, sir."

Casmir nodded, then strode on down the hallway to rejoin his entourage.

"Impressive as always," Yvonne said as they walked away.

"They just needed to be reminded of the goal," he replied as they entered the final corridor that led to the launch bay.

"That's why you make a better commander than me," she replied. "I would have just kicked their asses."

He laughed out loud, and her expression changed to a broad smile.

"There's the guy I know," she said.

As they continued, a robotic pallet zipped along programmed routes to haul more matériel into the mission craft. A trolley shuttle twisted through the hallway like a slalom skier, its gears whining with a low grate. They turned down a series of lesser-used passages, ducking past one of the many air locks he had demanded be built into the network.

He pulled at the sleeve of his uniform and tugged at his collar.

People had seen them earlier, but in just a few moments their party would come to where the escape crafts were being loaded and boarded. The show would get public then and he wanted to appear strong.

"Are you all right?" Yvonne finally asked.

"Yes," he replied with anger he was embarrassed of.

Yvonne's face darkened. She didn't deserve his snippiness.

"I'm sorry," he said softly enough that only she could hear.

Yvonne reached up and touched his shoulder.

He sighed and let his fingers drift over to take her hand.

"If you happen to have a crystal ball, I would love to know where we are three hours from now," he said.

Yvonne laughed.

"Should I leave you to walk into the launch bay by yourself?" she said as they came nearer the final staging passages. She let go of his hand.

He gave her a glance as if to say *what the hell are you thinking?*

"I just thought it might be best if people saw you—"

Casmir waved her off.

"I expect our folks will be more pleased to see you beside me. But I don't care one way or the other what they think right now. You've done as much for U3 as I have. I'm with you. You're with me."

Yvonne's chest rose with a breath, and she relaxed. She gave Casmir's hand a squeeze, then dropped it to straighten her own jacket.

Lines outlined her lips, and the gray in her hair seemed suddenly more prominent. Like him, she had put on weight recently, and he saw it as shadows under her jawline. Neither of them had kept their fitness as maybe they should have, but then, they had both changed from the early days in other ways, too. Despite that, she was still the same Yvonne in all the ways that mattered. Every bit the warrior she had been when they had first met. Her eyes still gleamed with purpose, and passion was still firmly embedded in the way she carried herself.

"Thank you," she said.

The soles of their boots echoed in the last few meters of enclosed space as they arrived at the launch bay.

Footsteps came from ahead. A cadet came to a stop before them, somewhat out of breath. "News, sir."

"What is it?" Casmir said.

"Defense systems report that our ground gun stations have been breached by UG guerillas."

Casmir looked at the guards, then to Yvonne. The government had broken through their perimeter and, presumably, taken out their outermost defensive positions. The response was even quicker than he had expected, but yes, it had been expected. Gregor Anderson was a very bright man.

"All right," he said. "Let's get going. We don't have much time."

CHAPTER 14

UGSS Carrier Transport *Ambassador*
Local Solar Date: March 14, 2206
Local Solar Time: 0505 Hours

United Government Interstellar Command pilot Alex "Deuce" Jarboe sat in the cockpit of his XB-25 Firebrand and tried keep his emotions in check as the plasteel cockpit slammed shut around him.

Despite the fervor of activity throughout the launch bay, the clamor damped to a low buzz when the cockpit engaged. He watched green-shirted enlisted push bomb carts across the deck, and maintenance bots roll along their programmed paths to the places where they would upload final mission profiles into their skimmers. The launch bay was a massive opening that yawned ahead and over him like a cavern built into the carrier's rearward structure. It was ringed by screens that flashed with a ticker tape of information that flowed across his vision and reminded him of the advertisements that filled up the scoreboards at football stadiums.

Jarboe scanned his Firebrand's controls. Screens of data flashed with blue and green radiance under his fingertips. They registered O2 levels, target coordinates, the programmed flight plans, and the charged power status of the two Taylor and Getz ion drive engines that he sat over. He ran the containment seal diagnostic and got back a green light. The sound of his breathing was thin in his ears. His hands were dry, but sweat ringed his armpits and made his back grow damp.

Sitting in a fighter-bomber just before launch was a strange sensation. So many people were nearby and so many people were involved in the mission, yet he always felt so alone.

It had taken nearly eight hours for *Ambassador*, a Solar System class carrier and troop transport, to get close enough to Mars colony to initiate the mission, some forty-thousand clicks from the underground tunnels that were streaming with Universe Three terrorists—specifically including Casmir Francis, their notoriously radical leader. Now that they were here, everything was up to Deuce Jarboe and the rest of his squadron.

Nothing would make him happier than to go down in history as the guy who removed that parasite from the registers of the living.

He watched his new wingman, Todias "Yuletide" Nimchura, strap himself into his skimmer.

Yuletide finished an adjustment, then gave him a perfunctory salute.

Damn right you'll salute me, Jarboe thought.

Nimchura was a headache he didn't need right now, to be honest.

He was not your classic problem child, not a pure ego-bloated hothead so much as a guy who didn't care a whit about anything unless it was directly about flying. But Nimchura had a Mississippi-sized chip on his shoulder when it came to being the best flier in the squadron. The two of them had tussled more times than Jarboe could count during flight school at Miranda Station, usually with a girl as the catalyst. Jarboe never cared much one way or the other about any of the girls, but Nimchura never seemed to tire of trying to put him in his place and Jarboe was always ready for a good challenge. After flight school, Nimchura became your standard-issue hot-as-hell flier who was pathologically unable to take a direct command and whose whining when things didn't go his way could border on the infantile.

Now, Nimchura was paying for his disregard.

In what Jarboe considered a valiant but misguided attempt to fix his fixation on being a wing leader, Nimchura had been demoted to a wing slot.

And not just any wing: Jarboe's wing.

Jarboe smirked at the irony, but he had to admit that as he was sitting here on eighty-five terawatts of plasma thruster he was happy enough to have Nimchura on his wing because the fact was that there wasn't a person born who could outfly the son of a bitch. Assuming they didn't kill each other in the process, Deuce and Yuletide could make quite a team.

The controller's voice came over the radio.

"Prelaunch sequence initiated."

"Roger prelaunch," he replied.

His cockpit display lit up with blue diagrams that outlined their position, and the taxi diagnostic flickered green in the lower right of his heads-up display.

Thoughts of *Sunchaser*, *Icarus*, and *Einstein* flashed in his mind.

He had buddies on those ships.

Every member of Regi Station, which was where *Ambassador* was usually stationed, probably did, which would explain the extra crisp essence of professionalism that seemed to crackle over the mission. Every member of the crew was working with a grim-faced sense of purpose. One of them had even hand-signed a rocket they had loaded on his Firebrand.

Remember Sunchaser, Fry Francis, the note read. Then the crewmember had signed his name.

Jarboe's memory flashed to Janie Lowell, who had been serving on *Sunchaser*. He remembered the night he, Buster Jones, and the wisecracking Janie had played poker with a group of cadets from Pleiades command. The deck had been marked, of course, but none of Pleiades had been able to prove it until it was too late.

He remembered Janie snarfing in her English accent as only she could as she removed the coated contact lenses that allowed her to read the marks.

He lost touch with her after their Academy days, but they were still tighter than family in his mind—certainly tighter than Jarboe's actual family ever had been, anyway. Jarboe's father was a spiteful man, and his mother was an enabler. His brother was a guy with no ambition, and his half-sister was happy to live off her string of boyfriends, who were, oddly, just as content to sponge off her.

The cadets in his class were different.

Every one of them would have hopped the first shuttle to Regi if he had ever needed them.

Even Nimchura.

Jarboe made it a point to never kid himself about the UG and its politics. He rarely understood exactly what was happening above his pay grade.

He understood family, though.

His family.

The idea that he would never again see Janie Lowell made his insides bubble over, and the fact that Universe Three was responsible for her loss was all the justification he needed to step into his Firebrand and point a rocket at Casmir Francis.

He sucked a deep breath and clenched his legs together, feeling his butt cheeks harden against the Firebrand's seat.

His Firebrand shuddered as munitions officers oversaw the loading of the last of the bombs and shut the bomb bay doors. The skimmer pad they rode on slid away. The launch bay grew silent.

Jarboe looked at Nimchura, who was doing his own personal prep.

"Avenger One, you are go for launch," a cold voice said over the comm channel.

"Roger that," he replied.

He gripped the joystick and flexed his fingers.

The automated taxi system took over with a solid *thunk*. A minute later they were sitting in the staging lock, first in line for launch.

The air in his compartment tasted of plasticized sweat.

The staging door shut behind him, and data from his panel floated like digital ghosts in a sea of absolute darkness. Outside his Firebrand, the vacuum pump pulled atmosphere from the lock, hissing like a wave crashing overhead.

Then there was silence as deep as the darkness.

The launch doors split open to reveal a star-laced curtain of faded blue light.

"Green for launch, Avenger One."

Jarboe toggled the comm link. "On my sync, Yuletide."

"Roger that," Nimchura replied in a sharp blast.

Jarboe couldn't help a smirk at Nimchura's professional

response.

The pall over the situation seemed to have settled on everyone.

Jarboe punched the catapult's Go button, and a moment later he was riding rocket boosters on deflection angles to turn the Firebrand into a looping spiral downward toward the Martian surface.

Nimchura pulled in tight on his right.

Jarboe's targeting system gave a beep as it locked onto Universe Three's compound.

Now the bastards would pay.

"I have target lock," Nimchura said over the encrypted channel. "Ready for atmospheric entry."

"Ditto that, Yuletide. Remember the *Sunchaser*."

Entry was standard fare.

The terrain below was orange and craggy in the fresh light of early morning. The slanted angle of the sun cast long shadows over the ground, giving the landscape a harsh, oversaturated sense that reminded him of the rocky foothills of the Mongolian desert where they had trained so long ago.

Their path to the target zone was straightforward and unimpeded.

Universe Three's antiair defenses were limited to a triangulated set of outdated ground-based laser units, two legs of which had been disabled by a prestrike assault thirty minutes before. Without its matching pair the third laser had almost no chance of targeting any individual threat, so it went into sluice mode, flashing its cadmium blue beam wildly across the sky.

Jarboe timed his pass to avoid the danger.

Nimchura also slid by.

The target looked like barren ground, but preflight intel reported Universe Three's launch pad was hidden underneath a few meters of crust.

"Roll left," Jarboe said.

Nimchura peeled away to put a row of chugger missiles into the area, ripping the lid off the launch bay and creating a cloud of smoke and dust that coiled upward through the thin Martian atmosphere.

Jarboe's heart rate jumped when he saw signs of a spaceport there under the crumbling rock as he lined up his pass. Intel is one thing, but eyes-on confirmation was the nuts.

"Damn right," he said softly. "Damn right."

He leveled the XB-25, and thought of his friends from *Sunchaser* as he released his chugger missiles to fall toward the spaceport.

Suddenly unencumbered, his Firebrand leapt forward.

The arsenal split into multiple warheads, and Deuce Jarboe pulled up on the joystick.

His aircraft rose majestically back toward deep space.

Behind him the target erupted in a massive fireball of orange and black.

Chapter 15

Mars: The Hive
Local Solar Date: March 14, 2206
Local Solar Time: 0535 Hours

From his place at the command station and within sight of the three Freedom Launch vehicles, Casmir watched the attack commence. On-screen, a cloud of dust erupted in the distance, followed by a muted blast and a rumbling that came through the ground. The Uglies were focusing on what they thought was the Universe Three spaceport, but they were wrong.

Thanks to Gregor Anderson's prodding, U3 had used that "public" launch system for every routine operation they ran. But in their earliest months here, he and Casmir had agreed to dig this alternate launch pad. It had taken three years, much deception, and greater expense than many thought wise, but today that preparation was paying for itself a million times over. If his mission planners were right, UG controllers would see the carnage their bombing run had created and would interpret the relative lack of U3 response as an indicator that their mission had been successful.

As another wave of UG fighters swooped in, a member of the crew stepped toward Casmir, carrying a folded triangle of cloth.

"The colors," the man said as he proffered the triangle.

It was blue and green, with a red and gold trim, an older model of the Universe Three flag of freedom from the time just after

Ellyn Parker's death.

Casmir took it. "Thank you," he said.

The flag would be destroyed in the launch, of course, but that didn't matter. Only a few moments were left before they had to board. He glanced at Yvonne, who came to his side. Holding the flag in one hand and his staff in the other he stepped to the main bay, feeling both the crunch of time and the invisible pressure of a thousand sets of eyeballs. Over the years, Casmir had learned that the art of being visible was in the way a person carried themselves: straight and controlled, walking with a sense of dignity and purpose.

As he and Yvonne made it to the center of the launch bay, the area grew hushed.

The bay was a huge, high-ceilinged cavern that had been dug out of the core of the planet, buttressed with arching beams of stone and metal spans that disappeared into the tall darkness like fading bands of light. The floor was smooth and even, polished to a glossy sheen. In the distant heights, Casmir could barely make out the mechanisms that would peel the rooftop back. A muffled cough echoed from the crowd.

The bay's lighting was sharp here.

The ceiling doors were closed, of course, but in his last moments here he imagined the sight of the sky above him, picturing UG fighters as they finished their missions, the plasma burns of their engines raging blue and purple as they flew back up to their posts.

Yvonne cleared her throat, and Casmir unfurled the flag.

We've come a long way, Perigee, he thought. *I hope you would be proud of us.*

Yvonne helped him place it ceremoniously into a hole that had been predrilled in the floor.

He took a final look around the spaceport, breathed in the sense of the moment, then took one corner of the flag and pulled it taut to expose the colors and the figure of the gold-clad climber as she reached the pinnacle of a pyramid.

"Perhaps someone should take a picture," he said.

Applause began, slowly at first but building to a crescendo before fading.

"All right," he said in his loudest voice. "We all know what's at stake today, so I'll leave the speechmaking for later."

He looked to the three spacecraft.

"Let's get to work and make this happen."

Ten minutes later, he stood with Yvonne and fifteen leaders of his staff at the base of *Freedom Three*. They all wore the light pressure suits required for flight, and each had pressure helmets open for the moment.

Freedom One and *Freedom Two* cut sharp figures into the dark background as they sat on two other launch pads. They were thick tubes, nearly a hundred meters tall and with pointed capsules that seemed eager to split space.

Every system had been tested. Every test had been reviewed.

Freedom One was loaded with the equipment, material, and science the organization would need to grow. *Freedom Two* carried workers and support staff as well as some of the command staff and the most critical engineers. More citizens and workers, the leaders and support staff, the people who analyzed the cosmos around them and made decisions filled the holds of *Freedom Three*.

They would launch in that order. Science first, people second.

His staff would split among the three vessels.

"Ready for retraction, sir," the voice came into Casmir's earpiece with a tinny tone.

Casmir glanced at the roof.

"This is it, Gregor," Casmir said to Anderson. He smiled despite himself. "Faceplates down, my friends. It is time."

He toggled his own controller, and the covering snapped into place. His breathing rasped inside his suit.

"System command," he called into the radio. "Please retract the roof."

"Retraction initiated," came the reply.

Mechanisms sprung to life with the sound of grinding wheels.

The floor vibrated.

Above them, the ceiling split into four pie-shaped quadrants. Early morning sunlight streamed in to form a simple X and then became a full circle as the four slices disappeared into the rounded edge of the opening's expanse. The natural light took the blue edge off the artificial illumination around them.

"It feels right, sir," Kazima Yamada said.

"How do you mean?"

"It seems right that the natural light of the sun would replace the light we made at a time like this."

And it did feel right.

Casmir couldn't help but feel the hugeness of the world around him then. He thought about Mars and its poisonous surface, its irradiated soil, and its craggy terrain. He thought about the fury of creation that was a never-ending cycle inside star systems. He thought about his father and his mother, both dead and buried on Luna. As the sky lay open above him, Casmir thought about the UG Natim complex on the other side of the divide, their greenhouses and their power plants. He recalled how it felt to stand on Perigee Hill again and tell Deidra the birthday story.

He thought about the moons orbiting Mars.

Their spacecraft would be gone long before Deimos rose tonight, but Phobos, complete with its oddly shaped Stickney Crater, would be orbiting just over the horizon as they left. Phobos was a much smaller rock than Luna, but its orbit was close enough that it appeared to be easily a quarter the size of the Earth's moon. A trick of perspective, these two moons.

Phobos and Deimos.

Fear and dread.

How much of human life was fueled by those two emotions.

Sunlight traveled down the bay wall as the roof finished its retraction.

"Thank you for that thought, Kazima," Casmir finally said. "If not for you, I would have missed it."

He turned to his team.

"It's time," he said. "Let's go."

As scripted, Casmir, seated with Yvonne in the control capsule, was the last to strap in. When he was finished, he gave a single hard swallow, then uttered the command. The piloting crews took over from there.

Solid rocket fuel lifted them against the Martian gravity well.

The first stage broke off after a four-minute burn, then the stabilizing trim rockets fired to keep them on course, nudging them intermittently one way and then the next. Natim's control tower radioed to deny permission to fly, but the *Freedom* pilots of course ignored their hails. The two UG bombers that remained from the attack wave diverted toward the launch vehicles, but it was too late.

Casmir watched a video feed as they rose.

The original launch pad was a blackened mass of smoking debris.

As the three launch vehicles peeled away, he looked at Yvonne and pointed to the black dots that were UG bombers skimming their way toward their secret bay.

"The animals have left the barn, eh, Vonny?" he said.

She grinned back, but her expression remained tense.

That was all right, he thought as datascreens displayed each of the Freedom ships' telemetry streams as they lifted themselves out of the Martian atmosphere.

Yvonne was his regulator.

He needed that. It was one of the many reasons he loved her so dearly. They were a perfect pairing. He was her optimism. She was his pragmatism. Without her, he would be a foolish blowhard. Without him, she would be an overly cautious miser.

Numbers streamed over the screen above them.

One more step, he thought as the shuttle moved into zero-g.

One more step and they were free.

CHAPTER 16

Freedom Three
Local Solar Date: March 14, 2206
Local Solar Time: 0615 Hours

The wait for intercept was the moment Casmir dreaded the most.

The three Freedom vehicles raced for a point in space outside Martian orbit on a proverbial wing and a prayer. Literally everything they had ever worked for was on the line. If intercept didn't come, the entire population of Casmir's Martian colony would be dead soon.

A fatalistic sense of dread covered him at times, so he understood how the others had to feel, too.

This is why he unclipped his belt and made his way through the spacecraft, doing his best to delight in the sensation of zero-g in hopes that his love for it might mask his own fear. Yvonne followed closely behind, pushing her own fears aside to bring her a message of hope to the people who were with them. She talked to one family about planting lettuce, another about how they might help set up a construction team.

She made him smile, and that helped more than anything he could imagine.

As Casmir made his way toward the back, he saw firsthand that Freedom transports were not designed for comfort. They were painted a stark white and gray. They were cramped and awkward, built of solid composite material, and designed to make the maximum use of every cubic meter. Beyond that, they had no method of creating gravity.

He talked to people, making jokes with them, giving them thumb's-up signs, and anything else he could do to keep their minds occupied.

They were afraid.

They were worried.

A few sat to the side, nursing nauseous stomachs and clutching the obligatory zero-g barf bags.

It all made sense to him.

"Keep your chin up," he said to one young boy whose eyes were as big as a full Luna from Earth. "We'll be fine soon."

When he and Yvonne returned to the forward section, he felt better.

"When will the shuttle come?" Wallace asked, holding on to a book reader that was playing instructions and examples of oil painting techniques.

"Soon," Casmir replied.

"Will we be going on your shuttle?" Deidra asked.

"Yes," her mother replied, as she caught up and buckled back in.

"Good. Everyone should see us all get off together."

Wallace rolled his eyes.

Deidra grimaced at him and went back to checking her appearance in the reflection of a nearby porthole, focusing on the acceptability of her pressure suit and smoothing the U3 patches on both shoulders.

"Where is Cash?" Yvonne asked, taking over the conversation.

"He's with his *girlfriend*," Wallace said, equally disgusted at his brother as he had been at his sister.

"We need to be ready when the shuttles begin to launch," Yvonne said. "It will go quickly. And Deidra is right. We should get off together, so I need you paying attention. We need to be ready to leave soon."

Casmir left Yvonne to control the preparations.

He took a breath and stifled a cough. The display was filled with data that depicted all the ship's operational parameters. It flickered like a heart monitor might.

Casmir didn't say anything.

Just scanned the display every few seconds, waiting for intercept, and hoping they *would* all be able to step off the shuttle together.

"*Freedom Three*, this is *Icarus* reporting," the voice finally came over the cramped cockpit's intercom. "We have you on-screen."

"*Icarus*, this is *Freedom Three*," the pilot said. "Copy your message. Preparing for transfer."

Then the pilot began to report status to his passengers, but Casmir was barely listening. He looked at the scanner and saw the electronic signature of the Excelsior class spaceship lying just before them.

It had worked.

Icarus, under U3 command, had jumped to their location.

An electrifying sense of relief filled him, a swell of emotion that bordered on exaltation.

Soon, *Icarus* would deploy its fleet of shuttles to ferry material and members of U3 aboard. The logistics of it all was complex, but Deego Larsi promised the process could be accomplished in less than thirty minutes—less time than it once had taken to build a human pyramid on Luna. Thanks to modern logistical engineering, the ferry shuttles would latch onto loading compartments, pull them off the *Freedom* transports in mass, then automatically shove them into receiving bays in *Icarus*.

Two passes for each shuttle and the transfer would be complete.

Simple.

Then they would light *Icarus*'s Star Drive engines, leave the transport shuttles behind, and enter a new phase of Universe Three's existence.

They would start with Eta Cassiopeia—a system where their astronomers said inhabitable planets almost certainly existed, three of which were already predicted and spatially projected.

"We'll have our own place soon," he said to Yvonne.

"We don't have anyone aboard *Icarus*, yet," she replied.

He smiled, but turned to Gregor Anderson.

"What are the chances a UG launch can catch us now?"

Gregor pursed his lips. "Not good."

Casmir knew his friend well enough to hear the "but not zero" at the end of his response.

The pilot turned in his seat to face Casmir and Yvonne.

"We should probably prepare for the shuttles."

"Indeed we should," Casmir said. "I will give the command."

"Why should we go last?" Deidra asked, the dark locks of her hair drifting in zero-g. "Aren't you in charge?"

"We go last *because* I am in charge."

Her face grew dark. "That doesn't make any sense."

"That's how Ellyn would have done it," Casmir said sharply, watching his daughter absorb the information. "The people go to safety first, then the leadership team, then us."

"Go easy on her, Casmir," Yvonne said.

"She needs to learn."

"As did you at one time, as I remember."

Casmir pursed his lips. "Touché," he replied.

Yvonne may well be the only person in the Solar System who could get away with that kind of comment without pissing him off, which was also among the reasons she was the perfect person for him. He relaxed and looked more closely at Deidra. She was going to be a great leader once she grew up, but now was not that time.

"Once we get settled, we can think about her training," Yvonne said, mirroring his thoughts before he knew he was having them.

A latching mechanism from the first of *Icarus*'s shuttles attached to *Freedom Three*'s rearward doors, the booster rockets sending shudders through the transport's structure that brought a few yelps and sharp cries.

Nervous giggles followed.

The second shuttle docked with another rattling clank.

Casmir imagined what the sight was like from *Icarus*'s side of the process—people and material on automated trim shuttles that flowed across the distance between the ships. He wanted to see the videos, though the sights couldn't match the majestic images he could build in his mind. A system of spaceships painted white and silver, flowing back and forth in smooth transitions—a ballet of its own form, like blood pumping with the mechanics of a metronome.

"Come," Casmir said when everything was collected. "It's time we head to the docking bay."

The third shuttle arrived.

Then the fourth.

Necessary or not, a security detail escorted the Francis clan to their pod.

The external door irised open to reveal the shuttle's internal structure. The pneumatic sounds of air-lock seals hissed through the compartment.

"Whoa," Deidra said. "It's beautiful."

Casmir smiled. He couldn't have said it better himself. Everything about the shuttle's design was smooth and sleek, which stood out in stark contrast against the threadbare efficiency of *Freedom Three*'s basic monotony. Seating was padded, and had automatic restraints that each user could control themselves. The ceiling was lined with a continuous video display that was currently flashing with a request for everyone to take seats before the artificial gravity system was enabled.

Once they were settled, even Wallace stared out the shuttle's porthole as the pod launched and the sleek-hulled *Icarus* came into view.

Casmir looked at Yvonne, who was staring intently into the darkness outside the other porthole. He took her hand to squeeze it.

"I think we're in the clear," he whispered into her ear.

She shook her head, but gave his hand a return squeeze.

This wait, of all of them, seemed the hardest for Casmir. It was two minutes only, three at the most, while the shuttle ferried them from the carcass of *Freedom Three* to the future inherent in the *Icarus* loading bay. But every second seemed to stretch for him. Every moment seemed to fold in on itself until finally they connected to the Star Drive's loading bay.

Doors opposite them irised open to reveal an air lock.

The sound of air streaming into the environment built.

Then the far doors opened.

"Welcome aboard the UGIS *Icarus*," a piped voice said over the speaker. "Please take your time and disembark carefully as the artificial gravity systems may be gently mismatched."

Finally, after all others had left the shuttle, Casmir, Yvonne, his children, and his entourage stepped through the bay and into the ship's corridors.

The lighting was bright enough that he had to blink several

times.

The air was fresh and clean.

Holo projections lined the walls with images of Earth and Mars.

The artificial gravity system was perfectly balanced.

For that moment he put politics and the industrially complex issues of the UG aside, and merely admired the beauty of something as miraculous as a spacecraft that could travel faster than light.

He admired everything about the moment: the expanse of the craft, the clean aroma of the service bay, the sensation of engineering and vision that had combined to make it happen. Everything. Everything about *Icarus* that there was to envy, Casmir envied. He saw that same envy on the face of every person in his circle, Yvonne, Cash, Wallace, and even Deidra.

It would be wrong to ever underestimate a people who could make something like this, he thought. But for now he merely enjoyed their efforts.

"Casmir!"

Gregor Anderson came near.

They clasped hands.

"We've made it," Anderson said.

"It appears so."

Casmir looked at Yvonne, then.

She was grinning, actually smiling wide with her white teeth glowing against the dark skin of her lips.

It was an expression that made him very happy.

Chapter 17

UGSS Carrier Transport *Ambassador*
Local Solar Date: March 14, 2206
Local Solar Time: 0715 Hours

They landed in tandem.

Deuce and Yuletide, Yuletide and Deuce: the two best fliers on station. They had been together today, working side by side as if they had never scuffled before, supporting each other like they were brothers.

The mission had gone like clockwork—simple and straightforward.

Despite their success, Jarboe felt no joy as he sat in the cockpit waiting for the bots to finish their postflight scan of the engine seals. In this moment of silent solitude, he decided that while he *did* feel better—good, even—the memory of Janie Lowell's freckle-faced cheekbones and crooked smile meant he couldn't bring himself to feel any real joy.

The cowling popped open, and he jumped to the ground.

A second bot set about scouring the XB-25 Firebrand's surface, looking for damage in the fighter-bomber's microstructure and making repairs as it found necessary.

Nimchura was already out of his machine and was removing his helmet.

Jarboe met his wing's gaze. "Nice shooting," he said, offering his hand. "You cleared a path I couldn't miss."

Nimchura clasped hands. "Glad you didn't screw it up," he said.

Jarboe nearly rose to the bait, but let it go instead.

Today was about paybacks.

Today was about victory.

Nimchura had done his job. There was no value in a dustup now.

"Now we take back *Icarus* and *Einstein,*" Jarboe said.

"Damn right, sirs," an enlisted said as he passed by.

Jarboe and Nimchura looked at each other for an awkward moment, then smiled.

Thirty minutes after the mission was complete, Jarboe was in the mess hall getting dinner when he was paged to the squadron room. There, the mission planners gave them the news.

Their intelligence was "incomplete," they said.

Incomplete was a word that Jarboe had long ago come to understand meant *wrong.*

The U3 spaceport they had bombed had been a decoy.

Casmir Francis and the rest of U3's leadership had escaped from a hidden site several kilometers away.

Their mission had failed.

Not your fault, of course, his CO said.

Keep your chins up.

And all that crap.

Chapter 18

U3 Ship *Icarus*
Local Ship Date: March 14, 2206
Local Ship Time: 1300 Hours

"This way, sir," Casmir's guide said, turning him and his family toward the lift station.

"After you, Gregor," Casmir said, waving Anderson ahead. "I assume you would like to see the bridge?"

"I wouldn't miss it," Anderson said, his face split in a huge smile.

The lift tube rose like it rode on oiled air.

"We're excited to have you aboard, sir," the anxious guide said in an attempt to pass the time.

"Not nearly as excited as I am about being here. This is a beautiful ship."

"Only the best for you, sir."

Casmir lifted an eyebrow, realizing there was no way the organization could possibly have built anything as grand as *Icarus*, better yet four of them. That could change now, though. The designs and service procedures were all in the craft's memory banks. Universe Three had engineers as brilliant as the UG had. All they needed was time and resources, both of which he hoped would soon be in plentiful supply.

The lift arrived and the door opened.

The guide showed them to the bridge.

"Director Francis," a man dressed in a blue United Government uniform said, coming forward to greet him. "It is an honor, sir."

"You must be Timmon Keyes," Casmir said, taking the man's hand.

"At your service."

Keyes's grip was firm.

The bridge was too huge to absorb in a single glance. Three rows of stations were arranged in a cascading auditorium-style seating, yet only Keyes and three others were operating the controls.

"It looks like it would take a battalion to operate this ship," he said.

Keyes's eyes lit up as he gave a close-lipped smile.

"Full bridge would be thirty-five, sir. But you would be amazed what just the four of us can manage."

"I am never surprised by what people who wish to be free can accomplish."

The smile on Keyes's face broadened.

"Thank you, sir," he said. "Let me introduce you to the rest of the bridge." He motioned toward the other three crew members, all wearing UG livery. "This is Lenny Tash, Brooke Nassir, and Katriana Martinez. They all played important roles in acquiring this craft. We have others on board at other stations, of course."

"My thanks to each of you," Casmir said. "Rest assured I will see you are each recognized for your service."

"Thank you, sir," the blond-haired Martinez said.

"Yes, thank you," Tash added.

Nassir just gave a tight-lipped nod.

Casmir looked at Martinez.

While the others were just as firm in their greetings, there was an edge to her gaze that he liked. He made a note to review her records. It was his experience that people with that edge were important. They believed in their mission with a passion fueled by something greater than pure ideology. They worked for the cause because the cause was personal in some way that others couldn't comprehend.

He turned to Keyes. "I think we should be heading home."

"Yes, sir."

"Then take us to Eta Cass," Casmir said. "And we'll see what glorious planets await us there."

"Aye, sir. We'll do that."

Keyes turned to Martinez and Tash.

"Set coordinates, and let's get this beautiful spacecraft doing what it does best."

The light show faded as *Icarus* fell out of jump speed.

Casmir Francis stood on the high pedestal of the bridge and watched colors drain from the view panel. The entire room stirred slowly, each person moving with silent reverence, as if not wanting to break the mood.

"The lights were magnificent," he said.

Keyes replied. "It's a phenomenon that stems from the way the ship disturbs the zero field between matter and antimatter. It's a very unstable slice of space-time. Break the link between us and the wormhole as we're moving, and it will collapse."

"What would happen then?" Gregor Anderson asked from his seat at one of the command stations.

Keyes shrugged. "I wouldn't really like to find out, sir."

Casmir smiled at him, then at Yvonne.

"Just when you think you control everything, the powers that be show you otherwise."

"Yes, sir."

"Do we have the planet?" Keyes said.

"I've resolved coordinates to Atropos," Katriana Martinez replied from below, where she was operating the navigation station. "Initial projections were off a bit, but the first spectral scan suggests inhabitable surface temperature, and O2 content. It appears we can confirm liquid water, also."

By common naming convention, the planet was known as Eta Cass b, the second planet that had been identified in the Eta Cass system, but a scientist involved in their discovery had also named the three planets in the system after the three Fates: Clotho, the spinner of a life's thread, Lachesis, the measurer of that life, and Atropos, the cutter of the thread. These were the names that stuck.

Casmir admitted he liked the idea of landing on Atropos.

Atropos would shear the ties between the UG and their Universe Three renegades. The name played to his weird sense of irony, independence, and inevitability.

A few members of the United Government's scientific community also believed Atropos was a good target, but it was not a popular opinion among them at present, which added to its attractiveness as far as Casmir was concerned. It was expected to be a vaguely Earthlike planet, though its temperatures were a touch higher, and early scans suggested it had both an oxygenated atmosphere and organic markers that spoke of fertile ground and potentially active life.

All the data they were receiving from the planet now was in line with what had been remotely determined, but Casmir saw the relieved expressions on several of the crew. Seeing, he realized, was believing.

"Take us there," he said.

The crew got to action.

The door opened and Deidra entered. His thirteen-year-old daughter's hair was now caught up in a single businesslike ponytail that hung straight down in the artificial gravity. She held herself primly and walked without haste to her father's side.

Yvonne put her hand on Deidra's shoulder, but Deidra edged far enough away that Yvonne merely stood beside her.

"Did you enjoy the display?" Casmir said.

"Yes."

"You don't sound impressed."

"It's just a show. Are we going to the planet yet?"

"Yes. I expect we'll be there in a few standard weeks."

"Weeks? Aren't we just going to jump to the planet?"

"No," Yvonne said. "We don't understand the controls well enough, yet, and we don't want to make a mistake at this point. After we really understand the system, maybe we'll be able to make that kind of jump comfortably. Maybe the UG would take that kind of chance, but right now we'll do it the old way—and intrasystem travel is different from Star Drive travel."

"I know that, Mother."

"So it will be a few standard weeks."

Casmir stifled a smile at the sound of the word *mother*. Until just recently, Yvonne had been Mama, and he had been Papa, but Deidra was growing up, and now those terms were occasionally becoming too young for her.

"What can I do?" Deidra said to him.

"Is your schoolwork done?"

Her face clouded. "It will be."

Casmir gave her a warning glance.

"I want to be a part of the landing, Father. Schoolwork can happen anytime. We're only going to land once."

Casmir felt the attention of the room. People were watching him now—which was good. That meant they were watching Deidra, too, and he was pleased to see her respond to that pressure in a way he recognized, sensing it and working with it.

He felt the attention of another young woman, too.

Katriana Martinez stood at the navigation panel, absorbing the situation with that same sharp-eyed expression he had seen earlier.

"Well, Deidra," he replied, raising his voice to ensure people throughout the bridge area could hear. "Your schoolwork is important, but I agree with you. If you want to formally join the movement, now is the best time."

Deidra's eyes sparkled. "What can I do?"

Casmir pursed his lips.

"Ms. Martinez?"

"Sir?"

"Would you be willing to help this young woman learn something?"

Her hesitation was brief, noticeable only because Casmir had been paying attention—a hesitation that he thought he liked. That pause said she was thinking through the situation, and that thinking said she had seen multiple options and selected the one she thought best.

"I would be happy to," Martinez said.

"Commander Keyes, make sure we get this new U3 recruit adequately apprenticed to the nav group, where perhaps her first exercise could be to witness the coordinate adjustments as Officer Martinez is working with them. Perhaps she can help your navigation commander ensure we make a clean approach to Atropos."

Keyes glanced to Martinez.

She seemed to be pleased.

"I can do that, sir," Martinez replied. "May we wait to begin until we get on intersystem guidance? That should be in a few hours. I need to concentrate until we are certain of that status."

"That would be excellent," Casmir said, liking Martinez more each moment. "Most excellent."

Deidra nearly shimmered with anticipation.

He continued speaking to both Martinez and Keyes. "Please know, however, she is to be treated just like any other cadet. She succeeds or fails on her own merit, just as we all have."

"Aye, sir," Keyes replied. "I understand."

"It's settled, then."

Casmir turned to his daughter. "You'll start working in navigation."

Her smile was almost as dazzling as the show *Icarus* had put on a moment ago.

"However," he continued, "as your mother said, we have weeks to prepare. So tonight it's homework for you. You can start working with our navigation specialist tomorrow."

Martinez was clearly pleased with the further delay, and Casmir was impressed that the roll of Deidra's eyes was nearly nonexistent.

With time to wait, Yvonne took Deidra off the bridge to get their personal items properly stored in her compartment.

Casmir went to Martinez.

"I meant what I said. Of course I want to hear how she's doing, but she succeeds or fails on her own. I expect you to hold her accountable for more than her name."

Martinez nodded. "Thank you, sir. That's what I would expect of you."

Casmir smiled, and turned, going to his own display of the local star map and adjusting it to show only Eta Cassiopeia and her four primary planets. It was an exciting system, fresh and pristine, open for them to set up the truly free society he always dreamed of. He glanced at the image of Atropos with its flickering screen of data.

Icarus would arrive at Atropos first and would manage the landing plans. *Einstein* would come later, after it had finished its work jumping back and forth to pull more Universe Three people out of the Solar System, starting with Io and Europa, then moving to smaller outposts where U3 operatives would gather in predefined locations to be extracted, and finally focusing on individual agents who had gone undercover and who were now holed up in safe houses and wayward hiding spots across the Solar System to avoid what would almost certainly be one of the more intense manhunts in human history.

Universe Three owed those people a rescue trip, and Casmir meant to make good on that debt. He and Gregor had been working on that part of the plan for years, setting aside funds to pay for alternate identifications, and to create urban safe houses in places no one would ever bother to look. The organization would pick them up in individual operations when the time was proper.

The crew, however, wasn't as familiar with the precision of the Star Drive navigation as they needed to be, so the process would be slow. *Einstein* would jump to coordinates they knew as safe, then motor on standard impulse to position themselves for rescue operations. Once on site, they would take on operatives, then jump immediately back to safety, hopefully before the UG could find them and run their own operation. So, yes, the rescue op would take time, but it would happen, and with luck it would happen more rapidly as they learned more about how to control the jump process.

Casmir stepped to Gregor's side and slid into a chair next to him.

His friend glanced his way, then took in the rest of the bridge.

Gregor's son was down working with Commander Nassir.

"He's a good boy," Casmir said.

"He's doing all right, I think," Gregor replied in his usual understated fashion.

Casmir patted his friend on the forearm and leaned back to glance out the observation window before turning to watch the crew chart their course.

As the younger Anderson worked, Casmir recalled how he and Gregor decided to take up Perigee's cause after she had been killed. He thought about Deidra working with Martinez. That was the way of it, wasn't it? The job was never really done, but the living and the young pick up after the dying and the old. Try as you might, a society was not a single life and a single life was not a society.

He suddenly felt tired.

"Life moves on, doesn't it?" Gregor said as he watched his son work.

"It does," Casmir replied. "But perhaps we can keep it from leaving us behind too soon, eh?"

He sat there with Gregor for a long time, looking into the expanse of space, considering for the first time ever what it meant that he might actually live to see a time when his people were able to live in true freedom, a time when Universe Three might finally have its own home.

Chapter 19

Chicago, Illinois
Local Solar Date: March 15, 2206
Local Solar Time: 1115 Hours

The notice popped up in Paul Kane's holo view. His senses jumped to full alert. Chief Intel Officer Matz wanted to talk to him.

He glanced at the time and gave one of his instinctive grimaces that was just a flicker of a reaction, a rising of the left corner of his mouth into a tight curl for that briefest of instants before it settled back to a straight-lipped expression of neutrality. He had grown this stoic form of expressing displeasure back when he played schoolyard lacrosse, back when the coaches made you pay for any outward display of emotion with laps. It was successful enough that pretty soon he was using it with his parents, his teachers, and his friends. The expression worked for him. It kept him on an even keel when he had to absorb defeat and gave his brain a few moments to spin up a defense.

The note from Matz hung there in his display until he dismissed it.

This wasn't good.

The Mars strike force had been misdirected. It missed the primary target and spent its force against a useless decoy. While that wasn't completely his fault, so much shit was going on right now that he couldn't predict what was going to happen next.

Kane was a man who liked certainty in every element of his life. He liked his calendar planned, his dinners charted out. He liked knowing where his people were. He liked understanding his relationships, and he liked those relationships clean and simple.

His office was small for his position, but the fact that he kept it spotless and he decorated it so sparsely made it feel bigger than it really was. His desk was simple, too, comprised only of a desktop that was a single large computer display, gently slanted to ease his viewpoint, and a stylus that lay like a gold slash in a marble tray along the right side of the display—an instrument that the president herself had personally given Kane.

Kane had fought for his place in this organization, and he would fight for it again.

The problem right now, though, was that while he felt the fog of war rising he didn't yet have a grasp on where all the pieces were.

He sat back from his desk, admitting this whole thing was beginning to make him more than nervous. He stood up and pulled his memory cube out of the slot alongside the desk. The block was light in his hand. He pushed it into his pocket. Its sharp edges pressed against his thigh with a certain satisfaction.

An unattended memory cube was a dangerous thing, even in the personal office of a branch leader of the United Government Intelligence Office—or perhaps he should say *especially* in the personal office of a branch leader of said service. Carrying the cube was old-school security, yes. But it was also old-school certain. *Carrying your secrets with you,* his dad had always said, *is the ultimate in security.*

Maybe it was his dad's tin-hat paranoia showing through, but the elder Kane had always been more concerned with things like double agents and internal espionage than he was with the fringy elements of external resistance, and that sense of paranoia had served to help his father live fifty years in the office and pick up a hell of a golden parachute on his way out. Given that the younger Kane could now cover himself by pointing to sensors and analytics, he expected it was about to serve him just as well.

He had no real concerns on the digital side of the security fence. His code junkies were topflight, so he would never believe any gaggle of independent software bandits could beat his team. But a memory cube was a cube, and if it fell into the wrong hands a memory cube could be made to sing. There were people here who could make interesting things happen if they decided to go rogue, and Kane was willing to bet his salary that there were rogue members in the organization who were closer to him than he would feel comfortable with.

Until now, for example, even Universe Three had been considered to be more of an annoyance than threat. But you don't steal a pair of Excelsior class spacecraft and kill another one without having tendrils in places that no one can see. Who knew where they might have people, now? This was why the skin at the back of his neck bristled at the sudden summons. He needed to be prepared to explain exactly how he was going to bring heat to U3 and how he was going to skim his own organization for possible moles. And now it looked like he was going to need to explain all of that before he had time to get his people together.

He collected his thoughts as he traveled the maze of elevator tubes and underground passages that led to Matz's office.

He needed time to get his people together.

That would be his play, he decided.

He would ask for two days, knowing she would then give him only one. He thought he could come up with a decent plan with a day to work with.

"The CIO will see you now," the secretary said as Kane walked up.

No waiting and no defined agenda.

More bad signs.

"Good morning, Paul," Matz said.

"Good morning, Sela."

He sat down, crossing one leg over his knee. A speck of lint marred his dark pants. He took a moment to brush it away.

Matz's office was larger than Kane's.

A bay window opened up to a view of the massive artificially lit, underground chamber that served as an emergency egress. The security offices had been built here in the late 2100s as a response to concerns about the old North American Federation's ability to withstand an all-out global attack. The cavern's walls were veined limestone with crystalline white patches of mica flowers that clung to the ceiling and glowed purple and orange in the artificial light of the passages below.

The CIO had been reading a datapad, reclining in her chair with one leg curled over her desktop, her foot covered in a dark sock that matched her pants. She withdrew the leg to sit forward as he entered, and waited patiently until he settled into his seat to place the datapad onto the table in front of him.

Kane recognized the data she had been taking in.

It was Pinot's work from some time back, with parts highlighted in light purple. Kane's eyes, like everyone on his staff, had been augmented years ago, but it wouldn't have been hard to read the highlights anyway.

"...heavy influx of equipment and material indicates possible tunneling activity," one highlighted section read. *"UG forces should be deployed to investigate the possibility that these signs are efforts to achieve additional surface access,"* said another. *"Perhaps geological teams could be justified without raising Universe Three concern."*

The date was three and a half years ago. Pinot had been an intern when he wrote it.

Kane fought an urge to run his hand through his thinning hair.

"Interesting in retrospect," he said.

"What did you do about this?" the CIO asked.

"I funded the Marikal op."

"Marikal was developed as a way to determine the quality of life in U3's camp, not to investigate surface access."

"We tried to get more out of it than that."

Matz motioned him to continue.

"Obviously, it didn't work out."

"It didn't work out because it wasn't designed to run that way. Would you care to try again?"

"What do you mean?"

"What did you do about Pinot's report?"

"We had other priorities, Sela. You know that."

"This hits hard, Paul. You know it, and I know it. The military brass are stinging because they just lost three Star Drive spacecraft. They look silly to the public, and they're ready to nuke the entire goddamned galaxy to get their revenge. We missed this one, and we missed it big."

Kane held the datapad and distinctly heard the *you* hidden inside the word *we* in both cases. He understood then that this game no longer had anything left beyond pure attack mode and the raw struggle for survival.

"We'll have to contain it, then," he said. "I can have a story out in fifteen minutes. U3 operatives found in the Interstellar Command hierarchy. We all know Francis had to have someone in place there to pull off something like this. It won't matter what we say—just that it's something strong enough to give us a day or two to breathe, then maybe get the president to talk about the Europa situation, tie in a renegade camp or two—kill two birds with one stone."

Matz pursed her lips.

He continued.

"We've been looking for something to take the wind out of the fringy elements out there for a while, anyway. So maybe we use this to make lemonade, right?"

Matz pressed a button on her tabletop display.

A holo-vid projection system rose up to cast an image of *Sunchaser* in the zone above the pad. An autodrone spoke in a chipper voice.

"In breaking news, Infowave sources report that Universe Three's covert activity to dig secret launch bases was known by those inside the UG cabinet more than three years before this devastating loss of three Excelsior class space cruisers. The ships, better known as Star Drives, had taken twelve years and 59.8 trillion solar dollars to develop—and that's on top of the eighteen-year round trip of the *Everguard* mission. Universe Three, a known group of renegade terrorists, destroyed one ship and captured two, then managed to avoid counterattack by using a previously hidden access tunnel…"

Kane stared into Sela Matz's eyes and knew what was coming.

"I'm sorry, Paul."

"It was just one report," he said.

She didn't move.

"We filed eighteen thousand reports just last year," he said. "You can't take me down for one goddamned report."

"It's our business to pick the mushrooms out of the shit."

"It's not as simple as that."

Sela Matz sat back and played her fingertips along the arm of her chair.

"There are four MPs in my waiting room right now," she said. "They'll escort you out. We'll arrange a time where you can come back for your personal effects."

Kane swallowed, and flexed his fingers.

"I understand," he said.

He stood up and turned to leave.

"You can leave your M-cube with me," Matz said.

Kane stopped, sighed, and reached into his pocket to withdraw the cube.

He rolled it in his fingertips, feeling the sharp edges of the crystal, then placed it gently on the corner of Matz's desk.

Without turning back, Paul Kane walked past his chair, past the side table, and through the door.

It clicked shut behind him with the finality of a dead career.

Punch

Chapter 20

UGIS *Orion*
Local Solar Date: March 20, 2206
Local Solar Time: 1300 Hours

Jarboe sat with Nimchura in the squadron lounge of *Orion*'s rearward deck. Neither one was particularly happy, but Nimchura was as testy as Jarboe had ever seen him. Turkey and ham sandwiches and a pair of mugs sat across the marbled plastic table between them, coffee for Nimchura, tea for Jarboe.

They were reviewing the mission plan.

What there was of the mission plan, anyway.

The flight colonel had just told the entire squadron that the intel geeks out of CIO said U3 was using their Star Drive systems to retrieve their people one outpost at a time all across the Solar System. The problem was, no one knew where they were going to arrive next, so the entire freaking flight group was going to loiter in space here on *Orion*, on constant alert until the bastards made an appearance—then they would jump to that location and commence to cutting up space.

"That's it?" Nimchura said. "We just sit here and twiddle our goddamned thumbs?"

"That seems to sum it up nicely."

"I'm sure you're fine and dandy with that."

"I didn't say that."

Nimchura glared. "Well, Number One, you wouldn't have to."

Jarboe shrugged and tried to chuckle, but the sound came out wrong. So he just sighed. "I don't like these phantom plays any better than you," he said. "Plans with no timetable are like football plays drawn up in the dirt."

"They're the goddamned wet dreams of conference room flyboys," Nimchura said.

Jarboe wanted to laugh at that one.

This kind of mission profile frustrated him because it meant they had to wait around until U3 just showed up, and even though Jarboe agreed with the expression of pure contempt on his wingman's face, jumping into their conversation full bore would just make things worse. He was supposed to be a leader, after all, wasn't he?

Jarboe scanned the mission profile again, which basically consisted of information about weak points of the Excelsior class spacecraft, one of which they were flying on now.

"It's like reviewing a goddamned fire drill," he finally said, deciding that complaining a bit couldn't hurt too much. "All geared up, and waiting for the bell."

Nimchura gave a grudging nod, which, to Jarboe, felt like scoring a clean goal in the eighty-ninth minute.

"It's the shitty part of being a space jock they don't tell you about in flight school, eh?" he added, pressing his luck.

Nimchura came as close to rolling his eyes as you can get without actually doing it. He crossed his arms and sulked.

The expression made Jarboe want to blow steam.

The guy was the biggest pain in the goddamned ass this side of Jupiter. Like a brick wall. Working with him was like perpetually taking one step forward and then a hundred-fifty back. He waited, looking around the flight lounge while his stomach acid settled.

Jarboe and Nimchura had come here directly after the brief. It was a smallish area, but well lit.

Its nooks and crannies were filled with plain furniture and just enough chrome and glass to lend the place an air of clean precision. The chrome was highly polished, the glass etched with 3-D images of several classes of historic spacecraft. The compartment's acoustically sensitive noise-reduction system made it an easy place to either relax or focus if you wanted to, and its open design in several places made it useful for gatherings and group events—such as the collection of pilots who were gathered for lunch, each group telling stories or chatting about actions or complaining about their dumb-assed mission profiles.

"Let's face it, Yules," Jarboe said, going in again. "We can look at this from the downside or the upside. And the upside is that we've got a way to find the bastards when they show up in the Solar System, so that means we'll get another chance to deal with them."

Nimchura squirmed in his seat. "Wonderful."

That seemed to be about as good as he was going to get, so Jarboe ate some of his sandwich.

UG scientists had used each ship's plasma signature to confirm that *Einstein* had jumped back into the Solar System several times over the past week, obviously working to pick up members at the bigger outposts of Io and Europa. They still couldn't trace the craft after it jumped back to superluminal flight, but they were now trying to identify patterns in U3's missions that might suggest where the bastards might poke their heads out of the quantum foam next.

While UG intel didn't have a goddamned clue on the whereabouts of any Universe Three outpost *beyond* the Solar System, they at least knew the locations of some primary outposts *inside* it. So given time, the political officers said they would be able to predict future U3 jumps. What that really meant was that they were putting every eye they had on the hundreds of known U3 operations centers, and that when a fish came into the net, they would ring up UG's military boys to jump *Orion* to *Einstein*'s location, then hit them before U3 knew what happened.

He wondered how much money all that observation was costing.

"Feels screwed up to be fighting *Einstein*," Nimchura finally said.

"Sucks skimmer dust," Jarboe replied. He took a swig of his tea. It was tepid.

"I assume they've got *Icarus* in on it, too."

"Probably."

To date, the intel guys said they could confirm only that *Einstein*'s signature was appearing, but he didn't see why U3 wouldn't use both craft to make these kinds of runs. That's what he would do, anyway, and the bastards were obviously not stupid.

The handheld projector on the table between the two men held the particulars of *Einstein*'s design parameters—defense systems, construction details, initial armament specs, and intelligence estimates of U3's ability to wield *Einstein*'s full arsenal. Nimchura was right. It did feel odd to be plotting an exercise against their own equipment.

Whenever it came, the attack profile was simple enough at its root—Jarboe and Nimchura were to escort a squadron of Kennard Aerospace TK-6500P troop transports into contact with *Einstein*, where those transports would then each dump their two hundred space marines onto the Excelsior spacecraft, who were then charged with overwhelming the terrorists and reclaiming the ship for their own.

They went over the particulars again.

Since they had no idea when the next jump would occur, it meant the squadron was essentially on round-the-clock call.

When they were done with this second review, Jarboe watched Nimchura to see how he was taking it now.

Which was still not well.

Todias Nimchura was certainly a helluva pilot, but was also still a total pain in the butt pretty much any time his own ass wasn't sitting in something that flew.

It was time, Jarboe thought. Time to fish or cut bait, as his grandfather would have said.

"What's chewing your ass, Yules?"

"What do you mean?"

"Don't play dumbass with me. If you're going to be an asshole, go all the way to full goddamned asshole. Just let it fly."

"Let it fly?"

"Give me everything you've got."

Nimchura picked up his mug and drank from it, setting it down with an amused expression on his stubbled face.

Jarboe set his own cup down, feeling the coarse grounds of his tea against his back teeth.

"You don't wanna know what's pissing me off."

"Are you going out for drama queen master stripes, or what?"

Nimchura gave a shit-eating grin. "You don't know anything

about me."

"Maybe I would know you better if you ever opened yourself up at all. I mean, shit, we were in flight school together and I don't even know where you went to goddamned college at."

"You want to know about me?"

"Just the facts, ma'am."

Nimchura gave a caustic laugh. "Just the facts." He shook his head. "All right, here they go. Simple and straight on. I'm twenty-six years old, with degrees in aerospace engineering and micro-g bio. I've never had a damned thing given to me, ever. I was born in Tupelo, Mississippi. My daddy didn't have any money bags strapped onto his hips. I worked a hundred grunt jobs to get through prep school. And now—after basic, and after ringing in at the top of the class in three flight schools—here I am, the best flier in the entire goddamned Academy, and still I'm sitting here flying right-side for you."

Nimchura stared at Jarboe full on.

"Satisfied?"

"Very nice," Jarboe said. "Your Momma and Daddy must be proud of you making the Academy coming from that kind a start."

"Momma and Daddy been gone a long time, buddy."

"I'm sorry. I shouldn't have pressed my luck."

"That's your problem, Deuce," Nimchura said. "That's all your all's problems. You're always sorry. Sorry for this. Sorry for that. Sorry for being in charge. Sorry for what the hell ever your ass is sorry for. You're all smart as hell out of a book, but you think everything you do will always wind up just fine, and if it doesn't you're just sorry as all hell that someone else got squashed in the process. You're a rich kid from a rich family who grew up thinking you can't do nothing wrong, or that there's no problem that a little money in the right pocket won't buy you out of."

"You don't like me because my grandfather made money?" Jarboe gave a wry smile.

"I don't care about that."

"Not my fault he made a jillion solars on Io. I wasn't even alive then."

"I said I don't care about that."

"That's bullshit. It's fine with me if you're an asshole, but don't go off on the moron trail or I'm cutting you off."

Nimchura shrugged. "Really, Deuce. I don't care about your granddaddy's money."

"Then what *do* you care about, Yules?"

"I care about flying."

"That's it?"

"That's it."

Jarboe waited.

"All I want is to be the best. I know *you* don't give a shit about that. You're a mission man. Follow the plan, do the job. Hip-hip, tally-ho, and a stiff upper lip. Stay in your box. Do that crisp barrel roll on command. But I say screw that. And that's why I don't like you. You don't press yourself. You don't take the chance. Who the hell knows, Deuce, you might actually be better than me, but you don't care about that so you'll never know. You don't even try. So stay in the system. Fly in your box. Stay at nine-tenths to keep control. That's your thing. But to be blunt, wing leader o' mine, when a time comes that I need someone covering my ass, I want to know they'll go ten-tenths to keep me safe."

Nimchura sat back and pursed his lips.

"So, yeah," he finished. "I don't like you."

Jarboe drew a deep breath. His wingman hadn't said that many words in a row since they had been assigned to each other.

"Why do you think they assigned you as my wing, Yules?"

"We're on the same side? Is that your point, Number One?"

"Seriously. Why are you my wingman?"

The silence between them stretched out.

"I would have to guess it's so I can learn from the best mission man in the system," Nimchura said, his tone dripping with an exaggerated southern drawl.

Jarboe downed his tea, then placed the mug back on the table. He was down to the dregs and the liquid was gritty against his throat. The cup gave a hollow sound as he put it on the table.

"Yules," he said. "I agree, you are the best pure flier I have ever seen. I mean that from right here." He pressed his closed fist against his chest. "No bullshit, pure or otherwise. Whether I take risks or not, I know you're better than me. But you're my wingman because Captain Galloway specifically asked me to help you get your act in gear so you can actually function as part of the group."

"Well, crap my pants," Nimchura said, giving an exasperated

sigh. "If that ain't a major-assed surprise."

"There's an example."

Nimchura edged forward, putting his elbow on the table and looking up to Jarboe with eyes that grew an exaggerated softness. "I'm sorry, Lieutenant Number One. I'm sorry I'm a better goddamned pilot than you are. And I'm sorry you have to carry me along as your wingman. You have it pretty goddamned hard."

Jarboe tapped a silent fingertip on the tabletop.

This conversation was just making things worse.

Across the way, a group of fliers sat at the bar, drinking. Another pair sat together going over their mission profiles. A collection of fliers stood at a vid table, playing a game of Kingmaker for a solar a country.

Jarboe clicked off the projector unit and slipped it into a slot in his flight jacket. Then he slid calmly out of his seat and rose up, straightening his jacket at the hem. He looked down at Todias Nimchura, who had an uninterpretable expression on his face, then twisted his body to face the entire collection of pilots in the lounge and raised his arms, palms up.

"That's right, Lieutenant Number Two," he said in a booming voice that rose in a singsong tone that echoed around the room.

Heads turned. Glasses were held in mid swig.

"I," he said, gesturing to himself, "am a crap flier—the purest of sheep's dung when I'm behind the joystick." He grew a toothy grin that was as comical as he could make it. "But I, Alex 'Deuce' Jarboe, am the chosen one!" His voice rose another notch and his fingers pointed upward as if he was a conductor. "I am *the man* because I *bought* my seat! Or, even better, because *my granddad* did! But you should pity me, pity me, I say! Because being Number One is a goddamned lonely job! There can be *only* one of us, after all, and that one is *me!*" He jabbed his thumb into his chest, feeling himself on a roll. "Me, I say! Me-me-me-me-me!" He pointed a finger at Nimchura. "You! Should love me for being such a crap pilot that the entire command structure can see how fantastic you are!" Then he scanned the room, pointing his finger as if it were a gun and jabbing it at every face he saw. "You and you and you! Every one of you! You should all love me for making you look like aces, my friends! Aces! Given that, I now so deign that you are each allowed to grovel in my vapor trails and pay homage…to me!”

He clenched his fists in victory, threw his arms out to his sides and his head back as if he was prepared to receive some kind of communion.

“Yes!” he called to the ceiling. “Yes!”

There was a pause, a beat of pure silence as the room decided whether Alex Jarboe was insane, an idiot, or both.

He straightened, then bowed to his audience.

“Thank you,” he said. “Thank you very much.” Then Jarboe adjusted his jacket again and sat down.

The room broke out in laughter, followed by applause.

Nimchura, too, was laughing.

“I never thought of it that way, Deuce. I’ll have to start a benefit in your honor the minute we get back from the mission.”

“I accept all donations.”

“I’ll ask them to be sent to SpaceJock.bank.”

“Don’t you think it should be SilverSpoon.bank, instead?”

“What an asshole you are,” Nimchura said.

“Singularity, meet black hole,” Jarboe replied.

Flight Colonel Meeds drew near with a tray of food in one hand, her Active Mission Control Protocol Indicator flaring green light down the shoulder of her jacket. If that shoulder ever turned red, the mission would be on.

“What’s going on?” the colonel said.

Nimchura answered. “Number One here was just explaining the finer points of cosmology, Colonel.”

The colonel stood there, her lips twitching.

“Great,” she said. “I’ve got transports to protect, and all I’ve got to do it with are a couple space jocks with as much sophistication as school kids.”

Jarboe straightened up. “We’re sorry.”

The colonel raised her eyebrows, but went on to find a seat.

As she walked away, grins spread across both fliers’ faces.

Chapter 21

U3 Ship *Icarus*
Eta Cassiopeia Arrival: Standard Day 8 (ECA 8)
Local Ship Time: 1540 Hours

Who would have thought that the most difficult thing about creating their outpost would be merely to get everyone to agree on where they should start?

Casmir rubbed his eyes and listened harder as the Universe Three brain trust talked over each other. They were meeting in the biggest conference center the spacecraft, a room just outside the bridge itself and just big enough to seat most of the group's better thinkers—Casmir, Gregor, and Yvonne, plus twelve staffers and three others. It was a sanitized oval space, with a white-topped table of composite material, and chairs all around, as well as a few standing podiums, which some of the members had chosen to use.

A projector system displayed a holo image of Atropos over the center of the wide table, its topography translucent but marked with data flags and colored in places that indicated more advantageous locations. Flyaway panels of data showed the computer's assessment of the availability of water, density of possible plant life, soil quality, and a hundred other different elements that the team was arguing over. The data grid was deep and intense, able to be resized to different resolutions at the wave of a hand.

The image also had hundreds of notes that had been added over the past four hours.

At first Casmir thought the goal was to prioritize landing sites.

Now he thought it was just to come out of the meeting alive.

The conversation had gone beyond the point of being testy thirty minutes ago. The conference room, which originally seemed so spacious, was now as stuffy as Casmir could ever have envisioned a session of the UG Interstellar Congress would be.

Kyleen Lian was talking. She was a biotech engineer by degree, with an agricultural family. She had spent years working with mold farms in the Hive and was clearly enjoying the idea of working on the surface for the first time in her professional life.

"The planet's southern hemisphere is in late winter," she said. "So by the time we can get settled there, it will be perfect for getting crops going and learning about the local flora. And the river basin at node six-twenty-three seems as ideal as we can get right now—plentiful water, reasonable grassland with some forestation nearby. It's also going to be easy to get landers in and out of. Yes, some of the soil quality measures are not where we would want them, particularly the estimates on slaking and enzymatic content. But neither of them are so worrisome that they should cause any real concern in the near term, and they could be wrong anyway. This is where we should go."

Several people around the table agreed with her.

Matt Anderson, who was participating in these conversations for the first time, spoke up. "The bigger continent has better plains lands, though," he said, motioning to a plot within the northern hemisphere. "We can plant there, too. Even you said that earlier. But the plains will be best for long-term expansion."

It was clear he was gathering support, though Casmir was now convinced that some of the room had come to back his opinion due to his last name and the fact that Gregor had been relatively quiet while his son did more talking.

Lian actually grimaced.

"Just because I see value in a location, doesn't mean it's the best idea," she replied. "Maybe we could look at putting an outpost there in the springtime. But if we use that zone now, we'll be fighting the teeth of winter before we can get seed in the ground."

It had been like this for hours.

Site by site.

Issue by issue.

Locations were graded for shelter, weather projections, potential for food sources, and a hundred other categories. The goal was a detailed plan, no later than next week. The team's preparation had been extensive, but was based on theoretical data projections. Now that they had arrived at Atropos and had real data, every topic had to be hashed out again, and as they were haggling Casmir saw interesting things happening in his team. They saw a future here. They saw lives changing. They saw opportunity. Reputations would change here, and Casmir watched them jockey for position in ways that he hadn't seen before.

He wasn't sure if this was good or bad news, but it made him uncomfortable. It felt too much like individual politics.

"You know what I think?" Casmir finally said, scanning around the conference room.

Conversation lurched to a halt, and faces turned to him.

"I think that this is a remarkable moment in our history."

He stood and stepped around the table until he approached the globe, where he stood and stared at the projection.

Its biosphere was so much like Earth's, filled with wild lands and water, oxygenated atmosphere, and almost certainly some form of animal biology. It was covered with rolling hills and thick forests. A huge lake lay in the middle of the planet's biggest continent. He could almost hear the water lapping at the shores.

"Isn't it beautiful?" he said. "Look at these islands." He used his staff to outline a series of islands that ran along the planet's equator. "I am old, and I am sick. Thirty years from now, I will probably be gone. Maybe fifty or a hundred years from now a majority of us will be gone, too. Maybe only Matt here will remain, eh?"

Light laughter filtered through the group.

"We have been working so hard for so long, and now here we are, talking about how Universe Three is going to settle the place where our families will be building their lives. And now that we're here, I think we're missing the chance to see this place for what it is. These islands, I don't think they would be a good place to start, but I admit I want see them some day."

He kept his eyes on the planet, but felt the pressure of gazes as he traced the islands again.

"I think some of the things we decide today will set the course of our history."

Finally, he turned away from the globe.

"That's no reason to feel any pressure, though."

The group reacted with humor, as he had wanted them to.

"I think it's best to remember these are not either-or decisions. We have time. Matt here, and many of you, and my own children will see a different world than we see today, that is for sure. Given a few years, we will put our boots down on any part of Atropos that we care to see."

He faced the group.

"I do not want to be a dictator. My voice is not meant to be the only voice. So along with this choice of what we do today, we need to decide how we actually make decisions as a whole going forward. Isn't this an amazing thing? For the first time ever, we can decide how to make decisions together rather than have to live in a world where companies and their puppet government set the course."

They were watching him now, glancing at each other in that way people have when they're seeing something remarkable.

"It will be difficult to figure out, but today we have only ourselves and our ability to compromise or argue. Today we need to drive to one point. So overrule me if you feel the need. But I think that now is the time to get safely on the ground before all other goals. I agree with Kyleen. I suggest we establish a place now where we can get entrenched quickly, and then I suggest we decide how we want to expand as the summer progresses."

Kyleen Lian beamed.

"Matt is right that we need to consider long-term farming arrangements," she replied, obviously trying to bring him into the fold but also helping ease the tension. "Agriculture is what will make us self-sustaining in the end."

The conversation raged on, but by this point everyone knew where it was headed.

Casmir returned to his seat and listened, still deciding if he should be ecstatic or if he should be worried.

Chapter 22

UGIS *Orion*
Local Solar Date: March 23, 2206
Local Solar Time: 0743 Hours

Nimchura checked the instruments as the XB-25 Firebrand came online around him, giving the signature shimmy and shake it was known for within the squadron. Graphs and figures flashed over his HUD. He clenched his fists and breathed deeply through his nose as the muscles of his back grew tight. He pushed down the edge of anger he felt every time he saw Jarboe in his Number One seat, and worked to inspect his wing leader's machine.

It looked fine.

He filed the visual report, then tried to filter out the rest of his animosity while he waited. Despite the fact that Jarboe was clearly trying, it was hard to sit in the Number Two seat and not feel at least a little pissed. In fact, knowing Jarboe was actively trying to be friendly just pissed him off more.

They were sitting in the launch platform.

Einstein had been reported loitering on the far side of the asteroid belt. *Orion* was going Star Drive in under a minute. She would loop across the solar dome at multiples of the speed of light to come at *Einstein* from galactic north. It would be some hairy-assed flying as best as he could tell. No room for error. But flying a Star Drive sounded like it wasn't his kind of thing anyway. More like pushing a cargo run than anything else, and who the hell cared about cargo runs.

Give him a Firebrand any day.

The launch window would open as soon as *Orion* arrived on site.

Anxious to do something, Nimchura toggled the mission profile.

"Star Drive engaged," the controller said. "Two minutes to launch."

Nimchura wrapped his hand around the joystick. "Star Drive engaged" meant *Orion* was superluminal right now, but since they were locked in the semidarkness of the launch port, it didn't feel any different to him.

"Roger that, Control," Jarboe replied, looking across the way at him.

He checked the blue and green readout that lined the edges of his faceplate, then the system parameters on Firebrand. All were Go, so he gave a thumbs-up.

"You've got two greens for launch from Red Squad," Jarboe replied.

Other teams checked off over the radio. The attack consisted of five transports and their Firebrand escort squads, but Nimchura tried to focus on his own machine and that of his wing mate.

He was used to people looking down on him.

That chip on his shoulder helped him compete. *Knowing you gotta be better than most anyone else if you gonna win means you gotta always push,* his aunt had told him one night before she died. She had lived a tough life, but she managed to get by and raise a bunch of kids, including, for the most part, him. That was the edge that had formed him. He was a winner. That's what he did. He had always won before, and he *should* have won this time, too. Jarboe could fly a Firebrand, but Nimchura was better, and everyone who watched them knew it.

But UG brass saw things differently, and now he was a Number Two, and Deuce "By-The-Book" Jarboe was Number One.

And he was not just any Number Two. He was *Jarboe's* Number Two.

"Dropping out of superluminal," the controller said. "Thirty seconds until launch window."

The power came up.

The automatic environmental controller circulated air, and the XB-25's preflight shimmy went away as the trim rockets kicked in. The door in the launch bay rolled open. Moments later they were flying, Jarboe a little above Nimchura's ten o'clock.

The transport they were assigned to escort was to their three o'clock.

The press nicknamed the stealthy TK transports "bumpers" when they were first announced because, they said, if you were in the target ship, you wouldn't know you were under attack until you heard a huge bump on the ass end of your fuselage. Training corporals called them "bump-n-grinds," to account for the sound their diamond-tipped drills made as they bored through the target's hull. The marines who rode them had a different viewpoint—they called the TKs "suicide tubes," because once all the bumping and grinding was over, someone had to run the hell out of the tube first.

Fliers, of course, had their own lingo.

From the distance of space, a bumper looked like a mosquito drilling for blood.

"I have our skeeter at three o'clock," Nimchura said on their channel.

"Roger that, Yuletide," Deuce replied. "We're right here with you, Bumper Three."

"Roger that, Red Squad One. Good to have you along."

They headed toward *Einstein*'s signature. If the jump had worked well, they would have a few moments before the ship caught wind of them.

Nimchura tucked in closer to Jarboe to give the skeeter and its two hundred lives a bit more room. Rockets burned, and the craft wheeled through space. The Firebrand's threat analyzer registered calm all around as he and Jarboe looped protectively around the transport.

Then, suddenly, *Einstein* entered his field of view.

An instant later, crimson and blue laser fire spewed from its rearward guns.

Shit.

Intelligence said those weapons were locked down under a top-secret code, and that U3 wouldn't be able to activate them for maybe as long as a year. So much for goddamned intelligence.

Again.

"Split right and under," Jarboe said in his usual monotone. "I'm going topside."

"Copy it, One."

The skeeter did its preprogrammed roll, and their scissors movement worked to confuse the laser's automated targeting code. Nimchura and Jarboe wound up together on the transport's opposite side.

The lock-on warning blared in Nimchura's ear.

He punched the joystick to tweak the system's preprogrammed evasive maneuver, turning it into a series of rolls and a crisp dive that wasn't in any of the evasion scenarios they had trained on. The maneuver disengaged the warning, but he had to pull up short to avoid colliding with the skeeter.

A cold beam of blue energy flashed past them both.

"You okay, Yules?" Jarboe said.

"Still breathing."

"Let's keep it that way, okay? You're going to get someone hurt if you keep improvising like that."

Nimchura grinned. "Jealousy will get you everywhere, Number One."

Einstein's flank loomed ahead as they went into their approach, the transport flying below and behind.

Nimchura targeted a launcher near the landing zone and squeezed off a series of rockets that killed *Einstein*'s external laser ring, but didn't breach the reinforced hull. Jarboe took out a second ring, but plasma flashed from *Einstein*'s fore-panel guns to burn away one of the skeeter's side boosters.

The transport rolled off the approach.

"We've got a runaway, Deuce."

"Copy that." The radio was silent for a moment. "Bumper Three, do you have a status?"

"We've lost starboard power and have limited attitude control. Working to restore. No estimate on timing."

"Get on top, Yules," Jarboe said. "I'll guide their right."

Nimchura grumbled.

This was a mistake—Bumper Three was damaged, and would never make the landing site. Instead of staying on the derelict transport, their protocol said they should peel off and support another run.

"Please confirm that order, sir," he said.

"I'm not leaving these guys alone," Jarboe replied. "I want you on top of this skeeter. Full defensive configuration."

"That's crazy—"

"I gave you an order, Number Two." Jarboe's voice was clipped but still in his lowest tone. "I expect it to be followed, thank you."

Jarboe dropped velocity and peeled off.

Nimchura gritted his teeth and fought the rock in his stomach as he stayed with the damaged transport, turning gently to stay above it, and from this angle was able to see Jarboe fiddling with his system.

Einstein loosed a salvo of long-range missiles toward their transport that Nimchura picked off one by one.

It took a moment to see what Jarboe was doing, but Nimchura shook his head when it became obvious. Deuce was taking the riskier and far more dangerous path of latching his own Firebrand onto the skeeter to serve in place of the damaged engine system. He wanted Yuletide to provide solo cover.

When he was ready, Jarboe drove his Firebrand alongside Bumper Three's side and matched its velocity. Then he tucked his nose cone against the transport and its burnt-out booster. Once the connection was made, Jarboe jammed the engines of his skimmer on full and brought the ship back to a course for their original landing target.

"You got a new right side, Bumper Three. Let's make it happen," Jarboe said calmly.

"Copy. Thanks from Bumper Three."

"Let's see those chops you're always talking about, Yules."

"Roger that, Deuce. And here I used to think you were risk averse."

"I'm a mission man, remember?"

Nimchura nodded, but didn't have time to reply.

He set program to run full-cycle patrol loops, essentially a continuous, corkscrewing outside barrel roll around the escorted craft that kept the transport on his bottom side the entire time. His threat monitors registered a new stream of combatants launching from *Einstein*'s holds. How good would they be? U3 pilots may be free-range good, but he doubted that they would have had much time in the seat of the odd little Z-pad skimmercraft they were pressing into service as fighters.

Bursts of radio chatter flew between Jarboe and Bumper Three as they exchanged the complex array of navigation and power commands it took to keep the skeeter on the proper path.

In the back of his mind it registered that two of the five transports had been destroyed prior to engaging. As they drew near, a third took a missile right down the gut and disintegrated into space debris.

Nimchura fired into the spread of *Einstein*'s Z-pads coming at him, making them sheer off to avoid damage. He broke left once to come around and defend the bumper's progress, then again to clean up a straggler. Both maneuvers drew fire, but he ran a clipper corkscrew after the first blast, and then a switchback on the second that put him into position to get rid of that fighter.

It broke his goddamned heart to kill a Z-pad like that, though. They were beautiful little machines.

He burned another of *Einstein*'s missile launchers near their bumper's landing zone to give the skeeter a free path.

"Nice run, Yules," Jarboe called to him as they settled in.

"Nothing to it," Nimchura replied—and he knew that was true. He could fly circles around these guys right now, but the fine adjustments he watched Jarboe turning as he guided the transport were the real thing of beauty. He would have to sit and watch the replay when they got home. The fact that Jarboe was making it up as he went, that there was no protocol or process for using a Firebrand to guide a skeeter, made Nimchura's blood run cold. He could look in the mirror as well as the next guy, and the fact was that Nimchura hadn't expected Jarboe to have that kind of flying in him.

They approached the site.

Nimchura rolled off to cover the backside while he waited for Jarboe.

"I'll give you a final burn, Bumper Three," Jarboe said, "then I have to roll out."

"Copy. Thanks for the ride."

The Firebrand's engines burned nuclear orange.

"Get out of there, Number One," Nimchura said, when he saw how close they were to the landing zone.

If something went wrong here, his wing leader would be a dead man.

He could be hung up and unable to disengage, or he could disengage too late and any one of a number of other problems could come about from that point forward.

Inertia rolled the transport right again.

Just before it made firm contact with *Einstein* Jarboe gave the skeeter a final blast of his engines, then peeled away. The Firebrand turned and twisted, but still it impacted *Einstein*'s hull, and the left side of Jarboe's skimmer crumbled. "Uhhh," his grunt came over the channel.

Nimchura looped over *Einstein* to see his wing leader was spinning out of control, headed into deep space.

Without conscious thought, Nimchura gave chase.

"What is your condition, Deuce?"

"I'm fine. I think. Just a little bruised. The machine is dead, though. No power. And I'm on reserve O2."

"On my way."

He hit the right-side boosters and rotated toward Jarboe's flight path.

The landing tether would have to do. It was probably a one-shot deal, though, because if he missed, it would take several minutes to retrieve the tether. Since his wing lead was on reserve O2, those minutes could be the difference between saving his life and turning the derelict skimmer into a coffin.

"Hold on, Deuce. I'm going to try my luck fishing."

"You're more good than lucky, Yules. Make it happen."

Matching velocity vectors, Nimchura launched his tether.

The attachment grabbed the derelict Firebrand's back cowling, and Nimchura slowed to bring the skimmer into control. It took several tense moments to temper the inertia of Jarboe's machine, but finally Nimchura was pulling his wing leader along like a trailer.

"Nice shot, Yules."

He turned on a slow burn to keep the Firebrand from becoming a total slingshot.

"Control," Nimchura spoke on the mainline frequency. "This is Red Squad Two. I've got a buddy tagging along behind me. Suggest you prepare the docking bay for a bit of a rocky entrance."

"Copy. Will have fire crews standing by," the controller replied.

Ten minutes later the docking bay loomed ahead.

Nimchura slowed to let the derelict Firebrand contact the back of his own craft. It was a hard impact, and at first he thought both fighters had been smashed, and then he worried Jarboe was going to slip off and crash into his left-side thruster. The connection held, though, and they flew tail-to-nose. Nimchura hit the retrieval motor, and winched Jarboe's craft up as snug to him as he could. He reversed the throttle to bring them to a slow, controlled approach to the launch bay.

It was a strange configuration to make work. He was pulling an inertial trailer wedged in tight, which meant as long as he made no sweeping movements, everything stayed steady, but as soon as he toggled the controls, Jarboe's Firebrand slid in unpredictable ways.

Nimchura made it work, though.

Half on systems, half by the seat of his pants.

"Nice flying," Jarboe said.

"I picked the idea up from a pretty good flier I know," he replied.

As they limped into the landing bay he hit the thrusters hard enough to bring them to zero-v. The bay doors slid shut and engulfed them in a moment of total darkness. Their relatively stable landing was almost anticlimatic.

"I owe you one, Yuletide," Jarboe said over the radio.

The words settled over him.

Jarboe had been about as interesting as a block of wood when they first met. He had that certain detachment from reality that seemed to cling to people who came from certain backgrounds. But Jarboe had a particular air about him that stuck in Nimchura's craw even more than the average rich kid. Nimchura was right when he called Jarboe a mission man. That's what he was. He was a guy who did the job, a guy who put the job first before anything else, and his job today had been to save the transport—and so that's what he had done.

And the fact is that the guy could fly.

Really goddamned fly.

"No problem, Number One. I think we're about even."

Then the lights snapped on, and the artificial gravity system took hold again. The sound of air filling the lock was like frying bacon.

Nimchura popped his cowling, and his crewmates scampered across the bay floor as he crawled out of the cockpit. Behind him, Jarboe slid to the ground and came around to the front, pounding Nimchura on the back as soon as his feet hit the floor.

"Guess we got the skeeter in there, eh, Deuce?" Nimchura said with a grin that he couldn't stop.

"That we did, my friend."

They were so caught up in themselves that they didn't notice the grim mood of the crew until a voice came over the loudspeaker.

"All teams prepare for immediate Star Drive jump."

"What the hell?" Jarboe said.

But Nimchura understood.

He had seen bumpers and skimmers disintegrating into balls of orange and red fire. The flush-faced glaze of the ground crew's eyes told him everything he needed to know. Bumper Three had made it in, but none of the other skeeters had landed.

A single team of rangers would seriously screw things up for U3 on *Einstein*, but they wouldn't win the day. The mission was another failure.

Now they were bugging the hell out.

Counterpunch

Chapter 23

U3 Ship *Icarus*
Eta Cassiopeia Arrival: Standard Day 8 (ECA 8)
Local Ship Time: 1600 Hours

While the argument was winding down, Casmir's comm buzzed.

He toggled the note onto his active sleeve and watched as the words scrolled past.

Einstein missed its scheduled jump.

It was from Deidra, who Martinez had assigned a role in navigation, but had been working down in communication and security as part of the crew monitoring *Einstein*'s jump. She shouldn't really have been the one to code the message, but Casmir wasn't going to argue about that right now.

The sentence made him deflate.

Einstein being late was nothing but bad news.

For a moment, he considered giving the whole room the brief as he heard it, but as the news settled over him Casmir didn't feel capable of handling the news in the same room with people he was supposed to be leading.

"Forgive me," he said, looking up to the commission before him. "But I need to take this."

He went into a separate room to receive the rest of the news, what little there was. While the Star Drive solved the problem of physical transport at superluminal speed, communication still worked in accordance with good old relativity. If *Einstein* was out of the system, there was no way to communicate with the crew. All they had was what they knew from their end.

"*Einstein*'s return jump didn't happen," Deidra said when Casmir contacted her. "The launch was perfect, and we're rechecked the return calibrations to ensure the multidimensional course codes were right."

"And?"

"They're the same set we've been using before. We don't think we're going to find anything wrong there. Everyone seems to think we should assume the worst."

"The worst," Casmir said. "Yes."

But what was the worst? An accident? An attack?

A simple problem with the science of the Star Drive?

Which was worse?

Was it worse to lose the ship to a simple accident, or have it damaged somehow and not be able to return? Did it matter? Yes, he thought. The latter could be UG retaliation, and that could mean a lot of things he didn't want to contemplate.

He sighed.

The worst case was this:

If the UG had taken back an Excelsior spacecraft, they would almost certainly be able to use the navigation systems and their calibrations to backtrack, and that meant the UG would know exactly where they were. He closed his eyes and flashed on an image of Atropos and the islands that lay scattered across her equator.

"Yes," he said to Deidra. "We can always assume the worst."

He broke conversation and touched Gregor's personal channel.

"I need you now," he said in the tone of voice that said it was important.

"Where are you?"

"Session Room Four. Leave the rest of the team to make the final decisions on where to land. Yvonne can shake any trees that need shaking. Bring Martinez, though. We will probably need to discuss navigation."

"On my way."

When he rung off, Casmir sat there, alone. Contemplating the perfect silence of the room's insulated walls.

He laid his staff across his knee, rolling it up and down his quad with his fingertips. They were so close. So close to being free of the UG. So close to having their own system.

With a final sigh, he activated the room's projector system and called up the same image of Atropos that hung in the larger conference center.

As the holo hung above the table, rotating gently, Casmir began plotting out what he was sure they would soon call a rescue mission, but which he was afraid might well set them on a course toward full-scale galactic war.

CHAPTER 24

U3 Ship *Icarus*
Post Eta Cassiopeia Arrival: Standard Day 8 (ECA 8)
Local Ship Time: 1630 Hours

They needed to understand what had actually happened.

That much was clear.

Casmir, Gregor Anderson, and Katriana Martinez sat around the small table and discussed their options.

Deidra was here, too, because Martinez had been with her when she was summoned, and decided to bring her along. When she first came into the room, Casmir had wanted to send her away. She was his little girl. She was too young. But she had to do this sometime, and she was learning fast. Maybe too fast. But observing how issues got resolved was good for her even if it made him feel like he was in freefall. She sat in a chair at the edge of the table, quietly taking the conversation in, logging everything that happened as well as any recording device ever developed.

Gregor radiated the same fatigue he had shown in their caucus with the expedition planning group. The last few months had taken a lot from him. His face was drawn and darkened now, lines marked his face, and rings had grown under his eyes. Casmir wondered if his friend was sleeping well enough. Gregor sat forward now with his shoulders rounded, his elbows on his knees, and his wrists angled against the edge of the table. Sometimes he made his hands into fists and sat his chin on them, other times he just sat back to think.

Martinez answered questions, but otherwise spent her time absorbing the situation. It was like she was calculating, deciding what to think. Casmir had looked up her records, such as they were. She had been with U3 for a long time, but working under deep cover for long enough that he wasn't sure how to help her, yet. But he liked her. He wanted to know more about what drove her.

"We can't figure out how to help if we don't know what happened," Gregor said.

Martinez nodded, but seemed uncomfortable in the room.

"We don't even know if she's a spacecraft anymore, better yet if she's ours," Gregor added.

Casmir agreed. "With luck it's just something broken. She's new, after all. But it smells very bad."

"We can't make the mistake of underestimating the Uglies."

A touch of surprised delight colored Deidra's face at Gregor's use of the term.

"I think we both know what we need to do, right, Gregor?" Casmir said.

His friend twisted his hands together, wrists resting on the edge of the table. Gregor looked at Martinez with a question embedded in his expression. "We need to jump *Icarus* into the area and see what's really happening."

It was a decision Casmir didn't want to make, but it was the right decision.

If this was truly a worst-case situation, they had to get out of Eta Cass anyway.

"Can we do that?" He looked at Martinez.

"We've got the coordinates and we can load the jump plan from *Einstein* pretty simply," she said. "Maybe it would be better to stand off a ways, though. Jump *Icarus* nearby and see if we can establish contact to find out what happened rather than hit the same place and run into an ambush."

"I like that."

"The ship's programming contains a few preplanned maneuvers that could be toggled based on what things are like when we get there, though maybe you should get a tactical engineer to review them first, just to be sure they're right. It's the UG we're talking about."

"How do you know this?" Gregor asked, his voice carrying a tone Casmir recognized as wary. Gregor was worried about her, he saw. His hands had stopped fidgeting, and he leaned back in his chair in a way that assumed a position of power.

"Security in the UG can get anything they want," Martinez replied.

A question grew on Gregor's face.

"Because that's how the UG is," Martinez added.

"All right," Casmir said. "That is the direction we go. Navigation will load coordinates near *Einstein*'s presumed position. We dip a toe into the water, and jump immediately away if we need to. One step at a time."

"When can we be ready?" Gregor asked Martinez.

"If we start now, maybe 2400."

"Then we start now," Casmir said. "Tell me what you need and who you need. I'll have dinner brought to where you are. Whatever you need. Just make it happen."

Martinez nodded, her lips closed tight. Her response, when it came, was almost a whisper. "I can do that, sir. Thank you."

She got up and left the room, Deidra following.

The door slid shut behind them, leaving Casmir and his friend alone together.

"Strange how time changes things," Gregor finally said.

"How so?"

Gregor gave a halfhearted shrug, and he tapped the table with the fingers of one hand. "Weeks ago the ability to work with even a single Star Drive spacecraft would have felt like the world was open beyond our ability to imagine, but after only a short few days of having two craft at our disposal, sending *Icarus* into harm's way feels like we are stepping onto a tightrope."

"I hadn't thought of it that way," Casmir said. He smiled then, thinking about how far they had come. "Enjoy it while we can, eh?"

"Yes," Gregor replied, standing. "Enjoy it while we can."

Chapter 25

U3 Ship *Icarus*
Post Eta Cassiopeia Arrival: Standard Day 8 (ECA 8)
Local Ship Time: 2330 Hours

Now they knew.

The jump to *Einstein* was flawless. Contact had come immediately.

Einstein's advanced firepower had staved off an attack, but the ship was partially damaged and probably not ready to jump back to Eta Cass for at least a week. In the meantime, they had taken a risk and used their standard impulse drives to dive into the deepest fields of the asteroid belt, thereby avoiding further immediate attack.

The hull breach from the attack transport was the worst of the damage, but it had been contained and could be repaired. They had lost thirty people in the battle, killed sixteen UG rangers, and taken four prisoners. Sensors that controlled the port-side boosters had to be replaced before they could jump safely, and several lesser subsystems needed to be restored. All in all, it wasn't the worst news possible.

Einstein should be jump-worthy in short order.

Icarus jumped to and from her sister ship eight times over the next three days, shuttling key personnel and materials back and forth, but always keeping their stays in the Solar System brief in order to prevent UG forces from finding her.

Einstein's laser defense rings were repaired first, her hull breach second.

Interestingly, the UG's presence in the area was minimal—two sightings of small craft.

"That makes sense," Martinez explained at one of her routine briefs of the leadership team. "The UG is cautious at heart. They've only got *Orion* left to them, and with only one Excelsior class ship, I don't think they'll risk her to the asteroid field. Especially not as a jump target. I mean, there *is* a lot of vacuum in the asteroid belt, but it's tricky to get a jump just right and if you wind up in the same place as other solid material, well, let's just say I don't want to be there when that happens."

Deidra had told Casmir that the woman had been spending all of her time doing deeper learning about navigation of the ships, and that edge showed in her conversation. "We all know there's a lot of space in the field, but the Star Drive nav programs are nowhere near as perfect as the UG wants you to believe. They won't risk losing *Orion* to a bad bit someplace, so if they want to go get *Einstein*, they'll have to do it with conventional equipment."

When it became obvious that the process was best left alone, Casmir and the rest of the leadership team left Captain Keyes of their own ship and the *Einstein* crew to complete their repairs, and they returned once again to the discussion of how best to run planetfall on Atropos.

At least, that was what Casmir Francis wanted to do.

CHAPTER 26

U3 Ship *Icarus*
Post Eta Cassiopeia Arrival: Standard Day 15 (ECA 15)
Local Ship Time: 0900 Hours

"We can't let this stand," Matt Anderson said. His face was now blotchy with the color of argument. He was standing, but leaning with all his weight on both hands against the tabletop.

The discussion had started as a simple update session where each of the Atropos coordination groups were giving briefs on actions they had completed. The initial landing teams had finished their surveying. Construction equipment had been dropped and tested. Shelter was being put in place and the area was in process of being secured. The teams had found primitive wildlife, forms of reptile and mammal, and insects—several strange forms of insects, some considerably more aggressive than those on Earth.

Theoretically, *Einstein* would be back in the Eta Cass system in a few days, and the work would then progress even faster.

They were close to having full boots on the ground, and the conversation was moving on to how to best use *Icarus* and *Einstein* as platforms for both education and expansion.

Anderson, however, was carrying a banner for one of the more active groups within the Universe Three community—and right now he was carrying it with a great deal of fervor.

Kazima Yamada responded. "We don't have the ships or the

people to fight an all-out war with the United Government. We've barely been able to salvage *Einstein*."

"Have you heard what the people in the decks are saying?" Anderson said. "We lost lives to that attack. They want justice."

"No," she snapped. "They want payback."

"Same thing."

Yvonne, who had been coordinating the conversation until the young Anderson stepped in, spoke up. "Justice and retaliation are not the same thing."

Casmir coughed, using his illness to bring everything to a halt for a moment. The ability to bring proceedings to such a halt was, perhaps, the only real benefit to being sick that there was. He was not above taking that advantage when he needed to.

Heads turned his way.

He raised a hand as he finished, then wiped his lips with a napkin.

"Dr. Iwal has told me I should relax for a bit. I'm sure everyone has either heard that or guessed it, so I'll tell you it's true. I need to rest. Vonny here has been on my butt to slow down for the past several days."

He smiled at her. She gave him a raised-eyebrow stink-eye, and the room got lighter.

"Of course, she's been too busy working with each of you to get us onto the ground to do more than wag her finger at me, so I've been able to ignore her pretty well."

More laughter came.

He stood up, breathed deeply, and gave another cough.

"I *am* tired, but I'm not ready to rest, because we are so close to the end game. You can taste it, right? We are almost to that moment when we can take a big breath of truly free air on our own planet."

He came to stand beside Matt Anderson, who stood straight now, anchored to the floor in a defensive posture. Casmir put a hand on Anderson's shoulder.

"Did we start this, Matt?"

"The UG started it by creating the wormhole drives."

"That's not a wrong answer," Casmir said, "but it's not correct, either. We are Universe Three. We take responsibility for ourselves. We have this conflict now because we are standing tall.

So it is fair to say we started it in that way. That's what the Uglies would say, anyway. And they aren't wrong. We believe things should be different. So we should never forget that we did our part to start this."

"Then we should finish it, sir," the younger Anderson said.

"Yes," Casmir said as he walked to the cabinet at the back of the room where coffee and tea dispensers sat. He pushed the commands for coffee and cream, and a hint of cinnamon added, then he turned and sat back against the counter while the dispenser operated. "We started this, so we need to bring it to an end. Of course we do."

"We can't win a war against the UG," Yamada said.

"Of course we can't."

"Then how—"

"The goal today," Casmir said, "is to get every member of U3 safely to Atropos without the UG being able to trace us. We should remember that—" Matt Anderson began to speak, but Casmir cut him off. "—there's more to it than that. We need both a new star system for us, and a pipeline back to the Solar System to bring in more people who want to live in a truly open system. That's the goal. Both a new home, and a paved road for others to get here. And so my good friend's son is wrong in his view that we did not start this, and right in his view that we need to be able to deal with the UG. We've been ignoring that here, and that's my fault."

"Miranda Station."

All eyes turned to Deego Larsi. The logistics planner, as was his wont, stood at a platform in the corner, an empty coffee cup on the stand before him. Larsi was a short man, maybe thirty-five, with a perpetual four-day stubble that he cultivated meticulously. He kept himself in shape. Casmir had listened to Yvonne complain about his penchant for being a smart-ass often enough, but he was also known for getting stuff done. Larsi understood how complex systems worked.

The dispenser finished with Casmir's coffee, filling the area with a spiced-warm scent, but he let it sit.

"What about Miranda Station?" Casmir asked.

"I think you're saying that once we get *Einstein* back, we need to hit two rocks with one skimmer, so to speak. That we need to take an aggressive act against the Uglies that will also serve to help us continue rescuing the rest of our people from the Solar System."

"Exactly."

Larsi motioned with his hand. "Miranda Station."

"I get it," Yvonne said. "Miranda Station has the flight academy, of course, but it's also a UG hub for the manufacture and service of skimmers, bombers, and other military spacecraft—specifically including *Orion* and any other Star Drive system the UG's ever made."

"Give the woman a prize," Larsi said.

"Yes," Casmir said, now understanding completely. "We've got people who say Miranda is most likely building at least one more Star Drive, too."

Yamada spoke. "Deego, you're suggesting we strike Miranda?"

"I'm saying that all they've got is *Orion*, which they probably won't get too risky with. At least not right away. And I'm saying that, as a guy who gets logistics, if—in retaliation for UG's attacking *Einstein*—you take out Miranda Station's manufacturing and service capability, then you also just happen to remove their ability to add to their Star Drive arsenal for a very long time—which then gives you something close to a free pass to pave that pipeline."

"I see," Yamada said.

Matt Anderson didn't look happy, but the rest of the group quickly reached consensus.

"I think it's a good plan," Casmir said, feeling that sense of power that happens when a group comes to the obvious answer.

All around him, excited conversation broke out.

Chapter 27

U3 Ship *Icarus*
Post Eta Cassiopeia Arrival: Standard Day 22 (ECA 22)
Local Ship Time: 1015 Hours

It took two days after *Einstein* returned to shuttle all nonessential U3 members from *Icarus* to *Einstein*—or to the surface. As the final shuttle prepared to depart, *Icarus* would retain the navigation and engineering crew, twenty staffers to handle weapons systems, and fifty people to pilot the Z-pad skimmers that would make up the attack force.

Miranda Station, named for its position in orbit around Uranus alongside Miranda, the smallest of the planet's five major moons, was so far away from the core of Solar System civilizations that the *Icarus* team could rely on a general sparsity of defensive systems merely because the station was considered nearly impossible to attack.

Until now.

Casmir ran his hands down his uniform. He usually played it informally, but today he felt the need to be crisp in his approach, so he donned the blue jacket with its red and gold patches and flaring.

"Let me go with you, Father," Deidra said, her face red with anger.

Now that she understood she had a place in the order of things,

Deidra wanted to be part of everything. She was upset that she wasn't allowed to be there while retaliation planning happened, and now she was convinced she was going on the raid with the Miranda Station team.

"No, Deidra. There is no place for you on this mission."

"Mother?"

"You heard your father."

Deidra screwed her lips over to the side.

"You assigned me to learn navigation. How am I supposed to do that if I don't watch the navigators?"

"You learn like everyone else—watch when they run test trials, pass your simulation exams, and then your own trials."

A knock came to the door. It was an escort.

"We're ready, sir."

It was time for Casmir to go to the bridge.

The escort would take Deidra and Yvonne to the last shuttle out, but as the leader of Universe Three, Casmir would be on the bridge when they made their attack run

He kissed Yvonne.

"Be careful," she said.

The pressure of her hand on his hip told him more than the tone of her voice. Yvonne was as excited about a life on Atropos as Casmir was. And, now, so close to the target of a potentially quiet life, she was more concerned than the part she was playing allowed.

"I will."

He turned to hug Deidra, but she was gone.

Twenty-seven moons plus the detritus from constant collisions of those moons meant their arrival at the jump target had to be perfect.

Perhaps it was luck, but the plan unfolded even better than Casmir could have hoped for.

With Martinez's modifications, *Icarus* made the close-in jump to Miranda Station exactly as diagrammed. The station was caught by surprise, and *Orion* was nowhere around to supplement its meager defense.

Three waves of Z-pad squadrons hit in perfectly timed maneuvers.

The first wave of the attack destroyed what rudimentary defenses the station did have. The second focused on the manufacturing lines, wreaking even more devastation on the chief areas responsible for cranking out XB-25 Firebrands. The third wave focused on the design center and test facilities at the engineering school.

The entire mission took just under an hour.

The destruction would cripple the Uglies for months, if not years.

As they prepared to jump back to Atropos, Casmir thought he might beam a message to the UG— something short but reasonably stated to suggest they could avoid a devastating war if they just left Universe Three alone, something that invited their people to join U3 in the Eta Cass system if they wanted.

Yes, he liked that idea. Not that the United Government would pay it any mind. But that kind of message would play well with the people, and he always needed enough of the people on his side. It was the people who mattered, after all. They were the ones who would use the pipelines his people were now going to be able to make in a nearly unlimited fashion.

In the end, though, he didn't.

Not yet.

Once his Universe Three was settled and it was safe to publicize their location, though, that's what he would do.

He smiled to see *Einstein* was in orbit when they returned.

It's over, he thought.

They had made it to Eta Cass in one piece. The UG couldn't find them. The war was done. The colony was free. The family was together again.

He felt a new essence inside him.

His mind went to Ellyn Parker, Perigee.

Then he turned back to his crew and began to direct their shuttle down to the base.

They had lives to build.

The Galopar Mission

Chapter 28

UGIS *Orion*
Local Solar Date: June 15, 2206
Local Solar Time: 1112 Hours

Nimchura pressed the targeting sequence on his e-lint system, engaging the atomic tagging process that latched the prototype rocket's guidance system onto the bandit skimmer. His breathing was controlled, his mind engaged and focused on the controls as his XB-25 Firebrand hurtled through space on full burn. A trim rocket along his fuselage fired staccato bursts of blue and purple plasma that snaked in trails alongside the machine's body and finally trailed under his cockpit. He banked on a hard left. Artificial gravity built in his spine as the Firebrand slid away, leaving the rocket to run on its own.

A moment later, the target was gone, and Nimchura released a breath.

"Bandit destroyed," he said into his intercom.

"Roger, Yuletide. You can shut her down now. Good work."

He sat back in the seat and flipped the switches that disconnected him from the program, then pressed the latch that released the pneumatic door. It rose like the wing of a bird, revealing Jarboe standing there with an impatient scowl covering his expression.

"If I have to drop another fake skimmer, I think I'm going to go crazy," Nimchura said.

"Time's coming," Jarboe replied. "Need to be sharp when it gets here."

"Nothing like optimism from the mission man."

Jarboe glared, and Nimchura actually stepped back.

"I'm sorry," he said. "I'm just kinda ready to burst, you know?"

"Yeah," Jarboe said as he stepped into the simulator to take his turn. "It's like dancing with a holo."

"So to speak," Nimchura added.

"It beats working with the press, though," Jarboe said as the door to the sim pod swung down.

"Burning my eyes out with a laser rod beats working with the press," Nimchura replied.

The door slammed, cutting off Jarboe's laughter.

Nimchura rubbed his hand over his scalp. He needed a haircut.

Jarboe could still piss him off, but the fact was that Nimchura saw his wing leader differently now. Not that it had mattered in the end. The failure to take back *Einstein*, and the destruction of Miranda Station's manufacturing capacity changed everything for everyone. *Orion* was being kept on alert, but held within the close confines of the Solar System to protect her against further attacks. Instead of actually flying, every UG pilot was assigned a half a thousand training missions inside sims and told that "something big" would be coming sometime.

Theoretically all this sim work provided the crew experience with new tech they wouldn't have gotten otherwise, and let them practice maneuvers with the high-precision jumps that interstellar war would require. Each exercise included hours of simulated skimmer battles, which, yeah, were good practice—time in the bucket was always valuable—but scripted training runs were dry as toast: Launch, fly around a bit, press a few buttons on a disabled weapon stick, then hit reset. All of it played with professionally clipped voices and hearty handshakes afterward.

Whoop-de-do.

He wanted to fly.

"Having fun?"

He turned to see Igrid Messier, one of Interstellar Command's press relations crew, and the contact assigned to manage Deuce and Yuletide's Ex-Comm—which was Command-speak for

External Communications, which was UG-speak for Meeting the Press and Answering a Bunch of Dumb-Assed Questions. She leaned against the doorway with one shoulder, her short hair staying in place as she cocked her head and appraised him.

"Hi, Igrid," he responded, knowing Jarboe had set him up.

"That was pretty good," she said. "I almost didn't see the eyes rolling."

The simulator made an airy screech that mimicked what a mission sounded like inside the cockpit. Jarboe was launching. The bandits would arrive in a few minutes. Nimchura wished the bandits luck, and considered bribing the controller to give the skimmers a couple extra atomic blasters.

"What is it today?" Nimchura said to her. "Kids in a hospital? Dogs need walking? A senator in hot water?"

Messier gave a smile. "Talk show."

This time he made no attempt to hide the rolling of his eyes.

Their time with the press began a month earlier when they gave a commencement address to the graduating class at LUMI, sharing the podium as Number One and Number Two, Deuce and Yuletide, the best fliers in the command: two brave pilots, competitors apart, deadly combined. Their story, Deuce using his Firebrand as a transport's engine to salvage a mission and Yuletide saving Deuce, glowed with a message of unity, daring, and honor that made even grown adults cry. The fact that the rangers probably did not survive was glossed over.

When the news cycle picked it up, talk shows began to ask for them.

The UG, eager for anything to change the press's focus away from inept war-planning and devastating losses, was only too happy to oblige. Soon Deuce and Yuletide were reassigned to doing commercials, giving inspirational talks at conferences, and air shows.

It was the first time Nimchura had ever been asked to do anything like that.

All his life had been about fighting for what was his, but now he had reporters fighting to get in front of him, and women, who he had rarely had great difficulty with before, now actively hunting him down. It bent his mind to read stories of dogfighting aerobatics that were technically impossible and kill ratios that would have made the bloody Red Baron faint. And at first it was fun. He learned how to use his Mississippi drawl to be endearing, and that if he let himself get excited some people thought he was happy to be there. But it didn't take long for things to get out of hand.

"I promise you," he once said to Jarboe after reading something called the E-Z-See Daily, "I never said an alien sat on my wing."

Jarboe laughed at that.

The only good thing about all the talking they did was that Todias Nimchura felt like he was slowly beginning to see the wires and ropes down inside his wing leader's psyche, understanding that Jarboe was just as frustrated with the fact that they weren't flying now, but that his wing leader could manage that frustration so that no one could see it. By seeing those wires and ropes Nimchura was getting an idea of how the guy worked—which he admitted was strange as hell, but interesting. More interesting, though, was that he was learning how to do a little of it himself.

It only took a few cycles to realize that PR work made them both need a barf bag, though.

No one else seemed to quite notice it, but he had grown to know Jarboe better than anyone else. He knew his wing leader was nearing a breaking point when he saw Jarboe snap at questions and get lost staring out windows in spaceports as they waited for shuttles.

The only thing that Alex Jarboe really wanted to do was to fly, and that was the one thing they most definitely were *not* doing.

CHAPTER 29

Washington, DC
Local Solar Date: July 6, 2206
Local Solar Time: 1115 Hours

It had been twelve weeks since Willim Pinot had taken Paul Kane's old job in the wake of the *Orion* and Miranda fiascoes. The news had not gotten particularly better, though the losses since then had come in a less public fashion.

Now Pinot sat on a bench, his business coat folded up beside him as he sweltered in the heat and watched a scattering of people move up and down the sidewalk. Everything from the sweat on his palms to the way the bench's peeling green paint clung to his pants made him feel sticky. He wasn't used to being in the field himself, but the opportunity had been too good to pass up. He had taken a tube into town this morning, and would be back home this evening.

The Lincoln Memorial was to his right, the Washington Monument to the left. They were remainders from the old world, as out-of-date as the idea of spending time outdoors. More decrepit statues and vine-clotted buildings stood scattered across his view, but Pinot quite honestly had no idea what they were, nor quite honestly did he care. Starlings and grackles moved across the lawns with the ugly motions that made him think of witches and sorcerers. The sun filtered through a few trees growing behind him. He was glad for that, at least. The wind picked through the hairs on his rapidly balding head. His tiny bag of popcorn drew a crowd of sparrows. Pinot put a kernel in his mouth while looking aggressively at the birds.

"Do they scare you?"

The voice came from a man seated on the bench behind him.

"Only when they cry," he replied as expected.

"Yet they only cry when called upon."

Pinot crunched another few kernels.

"Colonel Dembu," Pinot said, not looking over his shoulder.

"What do you have?" The military man's voice was smooth as vanilla bean coffee.

"All business today, eh?"

"I have a war to win."

Pinot, feeling it was wise to understand the people around him, had studied the colonel closely for some time and come to the conclusion that the man did not use this scarcity of words due to any desire to drive efficiency, but rather as a show of power. Dembu prided himself on the ability to wield words like swords. He swung his sentences in killing arcs that drew attention as much for their grace as their precision.

They could use more of that, now.

The news services may be full of jingoistic optimism and stories of expectation, but Pinot knew better. The United Government couldn't find U3 now, and even if it could its leadership was at odds regarding what to do about it. Without a fully operational Miranda Station, their responses were as limited as the wiggle room the political structure was giving them, and the vast remoteness that served to make it perfect for manufacturing the Solar System's most sensitive military systems was now serving to make it more difficult to bring it back on line.

Given the current political situation, though, men like Adubai Dembu were caught in the middle with a job description that read: Make it go away, but don't hurt anyone in the process.

"You've got leaks, Colonel," Pinot said. "Universe Three has been buying secrets."

The sound of paper rustling was the colonel's only immediate response. Pinot smelled the faint aroma of mustard and salami sandwich.

"Who?"

"I'm working on it."

"You don't know?"

"There's knowing, and there's knowing."

"Then what makes you suspect leaks?"

Pinot ate more popcorn.

"We know U3 acquired control of the ships by first accessing and overriding the security systems—which alone would require several sleeper agents. But they were also able to modify our laser defense systems much more rapidly than they should have been able to, and they understood classified navigation techniques well enough to sit down perfectly on Miranda. They knew enough to dump X-ray trash before a second jump, which makes it almost impossible to determine their eventual course."

"I see."

"So they've got people in each of those areas, and they've almost certainly been buying scientists."

"Engineers, too."

Pinot nodded and wiped his greasy fingers on his pant leg. "I suspect they've been bird-dogging every technology we've looked at for the past fifteen years. Maybe longer. Probably had an ear to the comm lines of half the influential members of Supreme President Mubadid's staff for at least that long, too."

"Hard to believe a fringe organization can pull this off."

The sound of the colonel eating his sandwich came through the breeze.

"You've been reading my reports."

"They're better than Kane's were."

Pinot smiled, retrieved a handkerchief from his pocket, and mopped his brow.

He had been telling people for months that U3 was not the tiny fringe organization they were categorized as by most analysts. This trail of reports had gotten him his position when Kane was canned. The more Pinot studied Casmir Francis, the more he admired the man. Universe Three may well be the largest single political organization in the known universe, yet Francis had both public and military opinion of his capability so deeply bluffed that the popular opinion said they were just another ragtag band of grease-painted commandoes that ran occasional pain-in-the-butt operations every now and again.

The storyline was that U3 had just gotten lucky this time.

Pulled off a one-in-a-million heist.

But, as the storyline went, now Francis had to live with his luck, and that was a different story all together. The big joke around the UG-shaped civilization was how absolutely stunned Casmir Francis was going to be when he figured out what a colossal mistake he had made.

Idiots.

Pinot waited while a father and three red-cheeked kids stepped past them.

"I know where U3 is," he finally said to Dembu.

"I thought it was impossible to track them."

"It is *almost* impossible to track them."

"I see."

"I thought that might interest you."

"How did you find them?"

"We all need our own little secrets, now, don't we?"

Francis was not the only person in the universe who understood how to use the "human" part of human intelligence, and Pinot wasn't going to out anything that might result in an agent left hanging.

"You found one of their agents?"

The sound of wind filled the place where Pinot's voice wasn't.

"Where are they?" Dembu said.

"I know the star system, but I'm still working on the exact details."

The bench creaked as Dembu shifted his weight. He was angry now. Not that Pinot blamed him. The cat-and-mouse game Pinot was playing was shitty.

"We've got soldiers dying out in space, son," the colonel said. "Do you know what the hell you're doing?"

"Details will come soon."

"I want details now."

"Soon," Pinot said. He ate popcorn and felt the bench shift under Dembu's weight again.

The colonel was getting ready to leave.

"That's not why I called you out here, though."

The bench grew still again.

"I'm listening."

"I've been reading about you, colonel." He rolled the paper bag up to seal the popcorn and put it on the seat beside him to give Dembu time to consider what that might mean. "We share certain opinions. We both know Francis has to be dealt with. We also share a distrust of politicians. We both know that if we do this in certain ways that it won't get done right because some grunty UG commando will find some way to screw it up. We both know that war on the galactic scale is going to be impossible to win, and even more impossible to get out of. So we both lose sleep at night because we know that if we just do our jobs, there will be soldiers dying out in space for the next several decades."

The colonel said nothing.

"I'm thinking that rather than go that direction, it might make sense to set up a team, let's say a group of military and intelligence personnel, a couple hundred folks, maybe, in a small base out there where U3 calls home, a hidden outpost near the terrorists' den that we can use as a central hub."

"That could take months."

"Maybe years," Pinot said.

He waited while the idea settled.

Star Drive ships altered the face of space travel, but now the next-generation cruisers—*Venture* and her sister ships—would not be built for years. And until these ships rolled off the production line, the UG had only the *Orion* at their disposal. Dembu was smart enough to know this meant that at best *Orion* could be theirs only part-time and only by wielding a great deal of political clout—clout that Pinot was pretty sure Dembu had just enough of—and even when they could win a mission, it would be a watered-down jaunt somewhere useless so that the craft was guaranteed to remain in service—unless that mission could be finagled just right.

Dembu was smart enough to know that despite the fact that the UG wouldn't take audacious risks with their only Star Drive craft, the distances associated with space were impossible to deal with if they didn't have feet on the ground in the proper systems. The career military officer would know instinctively that if UG politicians were to ever learn where Universe Three's camp was, they would fall over one another to be the first to send a mission to destroy it—but that this mission was certain to be a tactical loss, that Universe Three had Star Drive capability and an all-out attack was destined to fail and leave worse behind for the kids who were dying out in space to deal with.

Colonel Dembu was wise enough to know that the U3 were like cockroaches.

They had to be exterminated in the trenches.

Dembu would grasp this all if Pinot gave him enough time to think, and Dembu would understand that Pinot was asking for a single black op—a jump of *Orion*, a jaunt into the backwaters of some remote star system that could leave a small force of specially chosen men and women to address U3 on their home turf where their guards would be down.

"Can you hold up your end?" Dembu finally said.

"I wouldn't be here if I couldn't answer that question with a yes."

Pinot stood up and spoke as he brushed popcorn crumbs from his pants. He put his hat on his head and held his coat up by the collar for a moment before sliding it over one shoulder.

"If we find their home planet, are you in?"

Out of the corner of his eye, Pinot glimpsed Dembu's hat move as the old colonel nodded.

"Just find the bastards."

Pinot smiled as he walked away, already thinking about the air-conditioned confines of his office.

CHAPTER 30

UGIS *Orion*
Local Solar Date: July 15, 2206
Local Solar Time: 1112 Hours

The meeting was held in Flight Colonel Meeds's office.

The man who sat at the desk was as nondescript as it is possible to get. Blue suit, pressed. Pale collar, with a UG pin at the lapel. His hair was dark, his skin a brownish mix of ethnicities from across the system. His face was clean-shaven, his lips average-thin, and his eyes standard-issue brown. He sat without great rigidity, but with a simple posture that would blend into the background at pretty much any event one might, or might not, find him at.

Nimchura took an immediate dislike to him, but Jarboe just brought up a chair and introduced himself as they sat down.

The conversation was short and crisp.

Would they be willing to volunteer for a new assignment?

Yes, they replied.

It would be hard work, and insanely dangerous. They may not return.

Fine.

It might require them to be away for a long time.

Would they fly?

Yes, the man answered, his voice almost cracking the monotone. *They would need to pass a few tests, and they would likely never be able to talk about it to anyone, but it was important, and, after a time, it would require pilots with their skills.*

Then, yes, of course, yes.

Sign us up.

Just like that, Jarboe and Nimchura were the first pilots assigned to the Galopar Mission.

Nimchura understood the assignment meant a lot of work that was not flying, too, but he was fine with anything that got him out of the press corps and into something with space all around it. He couldn't help but smile, and the skin over his arms seemed to shiver with anticipation.

"I gotta go to the gym," he said to Jarboe as they stepped into the hallway that led out of Officers Row.

"Blow off steam?"

"Yeah," he said. "I'm pumped. You wanna meet there?"

Jarboe nodded, rubbing the back of his neck, then looked down the hallway. "Sure."

"Don't use up all that extra gung ho in one place."

"Sorry."

"Well?"

Jarboe's grin carried all the enthusiasm of a parent dealing with a rambunctious kid. "I'm gonna grab something to eat first."

"Good idea. Meet you there in thirty?"

"Deal."

Nimchura's smile was so wide he could feel it in his ears. The Galopar Mission was going to be brilliant, glorious even. It didn't even matter than he wasn't sure what a Galopar was.

Chapter 31

Galopar
Local Date: Masked
Local Time: Masked

A Galopar, it turns out, is a tiny shithole of a planet in the inhabitable region of Eta Cassiopeia B. Eta Cass B was the mate to the star system that Universe Three had chosen as its new home, and the smaller of the binary pair. The team immediately took to calling it Little Brother.

Unlike U3's planning for planetfall, the criteria for the landing site was simple: Find an open area with nearby water.

The drop happened in a single pass.

Fifty shuttles ferried engineers, ground support, and construction workers in via a single massive drop from *Orion*.

They brought in equipment and material.

Electronic assemblies.

Computer systems.

Weapons.

They dropped in material and components that would let the camp quickly assemble skimmers, rovers, and scooters. They shuttled food rations for several months, but assumed the group would eventually become self-sustaining. Medical equipment included antibiotics, basic first aid material, and other simple items—have a complex problem on Galopar and you were a casualty, but you knew that going in.

The whole thing—an entire civilization dropped onto a tiny planet—took roughly two hours. Then *Orion* was gone, jumped back to the Solar System to return to its patrol mission.

When Todias Nimchura stepped off the shuttle and onto the vast grassland, he had to admit it was one of the slickest maneuvers he had ever seen.

It was a strange and dangerous place, Galopar.

Overgrown with vines and thorn-laden thickets, and roamed by enough strange-looking creatures that, in certain other situations and for certain types of people, it might have been considered a paradise. When it wasn't cloudy, the sky was blue and carried a strange golden hue to it that made everything seem as crisp as a fresh dream.

It had been identified as potentially inhabitable years back, but dropped off the list of high-profile missions because other sites showed stronger traces of high-value metals. In other words, it wasn't worth it. Which Nimchura thought was a shame because the animal life on the planet alone would keep biologists busy for lifetimes. Not that it mattered, he supposed. But he liked vid-clips about animals, and he hadn't seen such a collection of actual wildlife since the schooldays when they saw clips of lions and antelope in the fields.

Little Brother was cooler than Sol, but at a distance of only .18 AU from Galopar, it warmed the planet well enough to keep its temperatures up both night and day. Its eighty-nine-day orbit around Eta B and its proximity to Big Brother Eta Cass gave Galopar an eccentric seasonal pattern. At about eight-tenths Earth's mass, its gravity was pleasantly low.

Very little of that mattered to the mission planners at all, who merely saw that the planet looked like it should be inhabitable, and that it was both close enough to the U3 outpost to support operations, and far enough away that U3 shouldn't be able to find it. The planners also didn't care that the planet's day was a weird, body-bending thirty standard hours and twenty-eight standard minutes.

Suck it up, they would say.

They were on Galopar to strike back, after all.

They were here to take possession of *Einstein* and *Icarus*, to show that no renegade group of terrorists would ever succeed in attacking the people of the UG. They were here with enough people and material to literally hand-assemble a set of Quasar transports to carry the platoons of UG Space Rangers who landed with them, and enough XB-25 Firebrands that they would also build themselves to support their raid.

It was the craziest thing Nimchura had ever heard.

He couldn't wait to get started.

Building a secret outpost that can assemble spacecraft, it turns out, can be backbreaking work. Doing so quickly, on a foreign planet, and under strict rules is even harder work, especially when those rules include such things as: All work that required anything with electronics must happen only in the hours when the camp faced away from Atropos. It was good security, they said—don't give the U3 bastards a signal to work with. But it was a pain in the ass, and it slowed things down to a crawl.

Vice Admiral Naomi Umaro, the officer in charge of the operation, was a hard-assed ice queen who expected eighteen hours of work a day and could manage to keep that pace up herself. She made it known immediately that violation of that rule was something you did not want to suffer.

Watching the base go together was like watching time-lapse photography. Generators were laid in a day. Command shack in three days. Mess shack in two more. Walls of corrugated composite laid against a wall one day were pinned to the bones of a training hall the next. Paths were cut, copses of trees cleared, roads pressed, foundations poured. The landing zone picked was mostly a flat grassland, which made securing the area against the indigenous predators relatively simple. The grassland fauna made dinner a time of interesting experimentation.

"I thought we were going to be flying," Nimchura complained at lunch after a week—which everyone agreed was seven local days. He was already tired of the work, and his skin was raw from scratching at bug bites he had picked up pretty much every night on planet.

Jarboe gazed over the horizon as he chewed some kind of dried meat. Sweat poured off his forehead and grime marked his cheeks.

His shirt blew in the breeze, but the breeze didn't help.

The humidity here made an August day in Mississippi feel like a treat. It rained every day since they had arrived—usually in the morning when cloud cover traveled along a range of hills that were almost mountains, and dumped sheets of water for about thirty minutes before the sky opened to blue.

Jarboe finally replied. "Captain says we'll start building skimmers and spacecraft once the perimeter is secure, and once she's sure we'll be able to keep everything safe."

"To hell with that."

"Still beats hell out of kissing babies," Jarboe said.

"Yeah," he replied. "I guess."

Nimchura chewed on his own slice of crappy dried meat, watching Jarboe from the corner of his eyes. His wing leader sat like he was conserving energy. He ate with simple movements, a straightforward swinging of his hand to his mouth, then back to his elbow resting on his knee, the shrivel of dried meat hanging loose in his long fingertips. His expression was bland and unchanging. Jarboe'd been quiet since he got here, and in truth ever since they had agreed to come here.

"You all right?"

"I'm good."

Nimchura waited, but nothing else came. Jarboe just stared out over the horizon and then at the walls of the shed they'd been assigned to build.

"Fine," Nimchura eventually said, ripping a bite of his own lunch and chewing on it with pent-up fury. Screw Jarboe. It wasn't like he was having any fun out here, either.

"Fine what?"

Nimchura gave an annoyed shake of his head. "Fine by me if you want to be an ass. I can take it. We're both all dressed up with no place to go."

"Hmm," Jarboe replied.

That was as far as it got. Which was more strangeness as far as Nimchura was concerned. In the past, Jarboe had generally been harder to shut up than to shut down. Now he just shrugged and ate.

It bothered Nimchura, but he didn't know what to do about it.

And in the end, it probably didn't mean much.

Jarboe being an indifferent ass was probably nothing a day in the seat of an XB-25 wouldn't cure.

More than two months went by before the "assembly line" even started building spacecraft.

More than two months of constructing sheltered buildings powered by solar generators and combustion engines that ran on wood and other organic material that was harvested locally.

Two excruciating months before the nearby forests were cleared of the aggressive animals that everyone took to calling saber-toothed tigers, even though they looked more like a cross between a hyena and a stunted rhinoceros. They got their nickname from the low growl they gave, but mostly from the curved fangs they flashed as they stalked members of the outpost.

Nimchura, Jarboe, and three other teams of pilots spent days pouring concrete for barrack foundations, concrete for storage areas, concrete for assembly stations, and, finally, concrete for launch pads. The afternoon the first launch pad was finished, they etched their initials in the composite.

Nimchura's back hurt, and his knees were knocky as he stood up that day, admiring the flourished T "Y" N that sat below and behind Jarboe's A "D" J.

It was good work, he thought.

Flat as a table. Solid as a…uh…rock.

When they finished the last launching pad, he looked up into the sky and could almost imagine a Firebrand taking off.

Four weeks after the assembly line started production, the outpost rolled out its first vehicle that could actually achieve orbit, a knockoff Firebrand that the gang called the XB-25 TriplePlus because they wanted the goddamned extra credit. They did their first equipment shakedown while the site was in its winter phase and Eta Cass B completely blocked its view to Atropos.

Jarboe got the first seat, using its maiden voyage to prove its orbital capability, a mission he accomplished in his normal, straightlaced fashion, with a stoic expression of duty on his face that didn't really surprise Nimchura at all, though maybe it should have.

Then it was Nimchura's turn. He nearly cried when he got into the cockpit.

His heart thumped as he sat in the seat and wrapped his hand around the joystick. He toggled the engines and lifted off from the pad. He was flying. Flying for what felt like the first time in all of eternity. And then he did cry, tears of joy flowing from the corner of his eyes as his head pressed back against the seat and the blue sky turned crystalline, and then black. He whooped and hollered inside the confines of the cockpit. He ran loops, like the flight plan called for. Then, rather than return directly to the post, he corkscrewed, followed by a sharp four-point compass roll. He dropped a quick competition turn, then a space-eight with a twist—which was his own version of the old Cuban eight—yelling out loud as he held the line on the opening and hollering like his aunt taught him when he finished it off.

It was only then that he saw the fuel gauge was drawing down.

A click of the system prepped the outer hull for reentry, which had the blazing brilliance it always had.

He set the Firebrand down just as its engines were sputtering.

Umaro, of course, grounded both their asses for three days.

Which they spent doing construction, joking, and stewing over the fact that they weren't flying. At least that's what Nimchura thought they were doing, until the third day when he realized Jarboe hadn't even reprimanded him for getting them dropped off the flight schedule.

"I'm surprised you're not saying anything about my dumbass move," Nimchura said.

They were building a pathway between buildings, and the sun was hot. Sweat rolled off their bodies and soaked their shirts, shirts they kept on to protect against sunburn and against the "mosquitoes" that were suddenly as thick as soup.

"You already know you screwed up," Jarboe replied. He wiped a grimy hand over his shirt. Then he picked up a trowel and got to work.

And that was it.

Nimchura focused on the work for the rest of the day, like Jarboe did, letting the idea that they were going to be truly flying soon keep his thoughts focused.

It was his fault they weren't in the air now.

He got that. Consequences, and everything.

But every time he tried to get angry at himself for it, he remembered his astrobatics and wound up smiling. And every time he smiled he realized the work they were doing felt good.

When he thought about Jarboe, though, the smile dimmed.

Something was definitely different about him, now.

Something wasn't right.

Three months.

That's how long it takes a small, dedicated crew of support specialists to build, test, and validate four Quasars and eight special Firebrands.

Now they knew.

Tack on another month for shakedown and testing of the pilot-craft interface, and you're about set. All total, the span from drop-off to mission readiness added up to nearly eight months on Galopar.

Nimchura was not going to miss it.

Especially now that they had been briefed on the plan.

The attack profile was ballsy.

The order of battle consisted of four Quasar troop transports, each carrying forty rangers, and each essentially ferried by a pair of XB-25 TriplePlus Firebrands.

The Quasars were stripped-down spacecraft, simple rockets that were throwbacks to an earlier time—launched into space on a set of powerful boosters, but not capable of complex flying. The Firebrands would lift off after the Quasars, be their primary guidance correction leaders on the subsequent flight, and escort them on the three-day, radio-silent burn that would take them to Atropos, where they would commence to whaling upon the U3 colony, a place they had started to call Atropos City. The satirical name felt right. Nimchura figured the U3 terrorists were probably living in grass huts, at best.

The Quasars would serve to refuel the Firebrands in a way that was similar to the old Supertanker in the Sky systems that had been so effective in the early days of primitive flight.

When they reached the target zones, the transports would enter the atmosphere, engage their stubby wings, and drop their Space Rangers on the surface while the Firebrands provided cover. The Quasar transports themselves would become bombs of a sort. The rangers would take out the ground crews, capture whatever Universe Three settlement existed at the time, take as many prisoners as they could, and use them to reacquire the Excelsior ships.

It was a one-way jaunt, succeed or die trying, dangerous from the minute it launched, a daredevil mission that, like the concept of refueling tankers, also harked back to the earliest days of flying.

Intense training had started over a month ago, and included three flights a day that were intended to create muscle memory for the act of jettisoning the Quasars—a maneuver made tricky because the transports were closer to gliders or old-time rockets than truly modern spacecraft in that they had only limited ability to control their own flight paths. The Quasar had been selected, however, because it was designed with stealth in mind, meaning each transport presented only slim cross sections that made them difficult for enemies to find. In addition, the Quasars' forward surfaces were lined with particle processors that took almost every form of energy its profile encountered and either reflected them away, or funneled them along its outer shell to exhaust away off the back.

A Quasar was nearly invisible to any sensor system ever devised.

A Firebrand, however, was not.

It was the middle of the night before launch, and neither of them could sleep, though in Jarboe's case that wasn't anything new.

Nimchura, however, wasn't used to tossing and turning. After a couple hours of it, he finally gave up and slipped out of his cot to head out to the front platform to take in the nighttime sky.

Jarboe was already there.

"What the hell is going on, Deuce?" Nimchura said.

Jarboe gave a motion with his shoulders that would have been a shrug if it had ever completed. "What do you mean?"

"I mean what's going on? I haven't seen you crack a smile since we got here."

"I smile a lot."

"Bullshit."

Jarboe just stared at the stars.

"You thinking we shouldn't have come here?"

"Naw. That's not what I'm thinking."

"Then what the hell is it? I mean, aren't you supposed to be the one mentoring me?"

Jarboe half-chuckled at that. He sucked in the strange Galopar air. "I don't know, Yules. Just…I'm…I'm trying to figure out why we're here."

"We're here to fly the guts out of a TriplePlus Firebrand."

"Yeah." Jarboe thinned his lips out, then brought his gaze back to the moment. "I guess I'm thinking a little bigger."

Nimchura rolled his eyes. "You've been reading too many news clips."

Pieces about *Sunchaser* had been Jarboe's favorite, it seemed. Nimchura had done his best to ignore all that. Yes, he was fighting to win, and the audacity of the U3 terrorists made him angry, but somewhere among all the construction and the training and the late-night conversations with Jarboe and the rest of the squadron, Yuletide Nimchura realized fully, and without any misgivings, that he truly was here pretty much completely because he loved to fly.

That was it.

Which, he supposed, was no great surprise.

"Maybe you're right," Jarboe said. "Maybe I am reading too much. It makes me think, though."

A flare crossed the sky—a shooting star.

Nimchura looked at Jarboe and saw he was struggling.

"I lost a lot of friends on *Sunchaser*, Todias. And we lost more guys on the *Einstein* thing."

"At least those guys on the skeeter went out like they would of wanted to."

"Did they?"

Nimchura wasn't sure what to say. He listened to the local insects calling, and bent to pick up a rock, which he twirled in his fingers. A growl came from the distance, but they both knew a guard would take care of it.

"Can't imagine they wanted to suffocate out in space," he said.

"Hmm," Jarboe replied, shrugging. "If we don't make it through this, I suppose there will just be another wave somewhere."

"I suppose so," Nimchura said.

"Don't you think about *Sunchaser*?"

"I try not to."

"Janie Lowell. I think about her a lot. She liked games. Anything that you had to outthink someone else. Now she's gone.

Just like that."

"Sucks."

"Yeah. Sucks. What sucks more is that I know she didn't really care much about Universe Three one way or the other. She was just doing her job, you know? Just doing what she loved to do, and now she's gone."

"You're gonna be fine, Deuce," Nimchura said. "You're the best flier I know."

Jarboe snarfed.

"I'm serious. You're a helluva flier."

"Yeah," Jarboe said. "I know."

They were quiet after that. Then Jarboe went back to the barracks, and Nimchura was left sitting in the darkness, looking up at the stars, and immersed in the music of alien insects.

Jarboe lay flat on his back on his cot, a thin sheet pulled up over his legs and halfway up his belly. His arms were raised over his head, hands clasped behind his skull. The buildings were not made to last. Their walls were thin, and the windows were merely stretched plastic. The quiet they held was really just a muted tone of chirping insects and the occasional wind that scrubbed that plastic.

He closed his eyes.

Nimchura meant well. He did. But he was fighting a game he didn't understand. How could he? It was a strange game, hard enough for Jarboe to understand, better yet convey in a way that didn't seem trite or petty. But it was a game, and it was an important game.

Jarboe had taken Nimchura under his wing. He had taught the guy something, he supposed. Nimchura seemed like he had matured a bit, was more under control. But what did it matter? What did it mean?

Nothing, really.

It turned out that Nimchura was right about him.

Life had always come easy to Jarboe. He was a jack of all trades, gifted enough to succeed at pretty much anything he decided to apply himself to. But that fact was that he hadn't really wanted to apply himself to anything. He didn't succeed because he loved anything—he had succeeded merely because that was what was expected.

He did the Academy like his dad.

Went to Flight School like his grandmother.

Took on Nimchura because it was his job. Even the thing with the skeeter: He hadn't done that because it was the right thing to do—he had done it because that was his job. Very pure. Very simple. You do your job, and you move on. That was his life.

Nimchura had said it all those months ago.

Jarboe was a mission man.

Then the UG sent them out on the talk trail and he had to carry the water, talk about the mission in that hyped-up tone of professional excitement, and listen to the commentators blather on about heroism and sacrifice, and he said all the right things because he had been so well coached and because that, too, was his job. All while his insides were rotting out from the memories of *Sunchaser* and friends like Janie Lowell, and from the idea that the rangers inside that skeeter were all dead now and probably would be regardless of anything he had done.

There had to be more to life than this, though.

More to life than being a mission man.

He didn't know what that was for him, but lying there in his cot that night, in a temporary barracks on a remote planet, Alex Jarboe made a decision that whatever that life was for him, it was starting tomorrow. It would begin when he woke up, follow him through morning ops sessions, and tag along as he strapped himself into the Firebrand he had helped build with his own hands. It would start when he did the prelaunch checklist, start again as he hit the Go Launch sequence.

Tomorrow, Deuce Jarboe was going to change. He was going to begin to live. Tomorrow he would begin a quest to learn about life, enjoy the moment, and to find out what he truly loved. Tomorrow, Deuce Jarboe was going to become more like Yuletide Nimchura.

The sense of happiness that draped him as he faded off to sleep was more alien than the grasses and animals of this planet, but it felt good.

It felt very, very good.

When Nimchura followed Jarboe into the barracks a bit later, he found his wing leader flat on his back, snoring like a lumberjack.

They were ready, he thought.

Tomorrow, the UG was going to strike back right where Universe Three lived.

CHAPTER 32

Galopar
Local Date: Masked
Local Time: Masked

Nimchura stepped into the hover that would take them to the launch pad and stood next to Jarboe. He cradled his flight helmet in the crook of one arm and held onto the balance bar with the other. The entire hover had been covered with a uniform layer of gray-blue paint to prevent rust—which would have made sense if they were actually going to be there for any real time—including the floorboard, which was already scarred up and peeling. Little Brother had been up for over an hour, making Nimchura squint at the horizon as he took his place.

"Don't forget to leave the light on," Jarboe said to the driver.

"Yes, sir," the driver said.

Jarboe looked at Nimchura and finally cracked a smile.

The craft lurched away. Rather than carry his flight helmet, Jarboe had put it on and left the restraint dangling and his visor in the up position. He held the balance bar with both hands, feet spread, and levered himself left and right as the hovercraft made its turns.

"You look a little like a kid in a coaster park," Nimchura said.

"Maybe I am," Jarboe said.

"Good dreams last night?"

"Good enough."

Nimchura braced against the last turn. He didn't care why Jarboe had woken up in this frame of mind, he was just happy to have the more stable wing leader back. Momentary grade-schooler aside, Jarboe had been his old self from the moment they met for breakfast and the final mission brief. He wore his old calmness about him today, a sense of oneness with the world that made everything else seem right.

As the hover straightened up, their Firebrands loomed ahead, standing in liftoff configuration, their noses pointed up into a cloudless blue sky. A single tech stood below each one, running final calibrations and prognostic checks.

It was finally time.

The last of the Quasars launched five minutes earlier. They would now catch up, and get the pack turned toward Atropos.

"Time to get in the chute, eh?" Jarboe said.

Nimchura nodded.

"Doing all right, Yules?"

"Yeah, I'm fine."

Nimchura climbed into his machine, settled into his skyward-facing seat, and toggled all the preflight checks. Green and blue lights fired up across all the controllers. The hydraulic lifters cycled the air surface controllers for their final tests. The cockpit was stuffy and humid until the air handling kicked on. Then it was cold, and his breath fogged the plasteel cowling that loomed over him. His skin tingled with the usual thrill of being behind the stick of a high-performance spacecraft, but he also felt the claustrophobic sense of being alone and encased in a dark metal compartment.

He looked at the displays as they came up.

Everything was fine.

"I'm good to go, Deuce," he said into their channel.

"We have green for launch," Jarboe said to the controller.

Nimchura put his hand on the joystick and played the mission over in his head.

If their intel was right, *Icarus* was likely to be stationed over Atropos City right now. At least they should plan it that way, and if it turned out not to be true, all the better. But UG's data on the terrorists' operations said they would leave one of the Star Drives in orbit over their settlement, and use the other for sorties. It was an idea that made sense to Nimchura—U3 were evil, not stupid.

The mission profile called for them to approach from the east, and if everything went well they would be in and out of at least their first pass before U3 skimmers had a chance to scramble.

He wondered what the encampment would be like. U3 had a few thousand people at their disposal, and he had already seen firsthand what a few hundred were capable of building in less time than U3'd had. After thinking a bit, he realized it didn't really matter.

Atropos "City" was going to be destroyed.

They had surprise on their side, so it should be a breeze.

A piece of cake.

"Vengeance Group Red, you have Go for mission."

"Let's do it, Yules," Jarboe said.

Achieving escape velocity was as exhilarating as always. A fist-hard crunch of weight on chest and a sense of gravity that pushed blood into places you didn't think it ever went. Then, suddenly he was floating in space and the plasma engines kicked in, and things were all back in place again.

"Give me a full burn on my mark, Yuletide."

The tone of Jarboe's voice was like hearing from an old friend. Nimchura had been right. Jarboe's bout with whatever he was bouting with was nothing a real job couldn't cure.

"Prepared to give you the burn, Mission Man," Nimchura replied with a grin.

"You're sounding pretty sprightly there, Yules. You okay?"

Nimchura hesitated, almost rising to his wing leader's bait.

"I got your right, Deuce. Don't ever doubt that."

"Roger on the no doubt. Let's go get us a Quasar."

Someone, somewhere, said that war is mind-numbing boredom interrupted by periods of sheer terror. Whoever said that got the boredom part exactly right. Three local days spent in the cockpit of a Firebrand, seventy–five local hours, to be precise, is a long goddamned time.

Through that time, Nimchura and Jarboe towed their Quasar, and all they had to look at were the stars, their ever-present control readout, and a seven-centimeter by six-centimeter display that had been rigged to play movies or shows. At least there was that.

They slept in staggered periods, though Nimchura mostly zoned at best.

He discovered that he loved the feeling of being in a gray state inside the cockpit, though. It felt like he was connected to everything at once, his body flowing out into every cubic centimeter of the vehicle, over servos and through wiring, into the metal traces that ran across circuit boards, and through optical processors that shaped light into collinear flows that became processed into information. His nervous system felt the pulsing stream of electrons that were keeping his spacecraft operational, the sound of the Taylor and Getz engines reverberating through the frame of the spacecraft to give it a feeling like it was his entire world.

But the rest of the time was just that—boredom. Radio silence meant the Firebrand pilots couldn't even break it by chatting with each other.

Occasionally he would put eyes on the Quasar behind them.

At least he wasn't stuck in one of those pieces of shit. He couldn't imagine what it would be like to be locked into a floating tin can with thirty-nine other soldiers for three days.

No, he corrected himself. For seventy-five hours.

Seventy-five very long hours.

As they came upon Atropos, the curve of the planet filled his view. It was beautiful in its own way, blue and orange that faded to a brown storm front below them.

Nimchura's blood pumped like a locomotive.

"Vengeance Q Red, we are Go for release," Jarboe said over the radio. It was the first live voice Nimchura had heard since the launch.

"Roger that, Vengeance Group Red Leader," their Quasar replied. "We have forty more than ready for release."

Nimchura was too busy coordinating his own release point to find humor in the Quasar's message, though, yes, he could well imagine forty rangers were more than ready to get the hell out of that transport pod.

They kicked the Firebrands in tandem and the Quasar was free.

It immediately began firing trim rockets to put it on a direct course to entry.

"Burn on three," Jarboe said.

"On your three," Nimchura replied.

Then they were racing through space, preparing an entry maneuver that would take them into this foreign planet's atmosphere. They would make the first passes on the settlement, scouting for big guns and taking them out. Protecting those forty rangers that they had just carted across space for three days.

"Roll down," Jarboe said, hitting the burn.

Nimchura whooped as he matched Jarboe's precisely made roll as they dived toward the planet. The upper atmosphere scrubbed white noise into the cockpit. Heat shields shed plasma trails. The ex-temp gauge rose within acceptable parameters as a fiery cone built on the nose of his Firebrand.

They broke the planet's ionosphere with a sudden burst, and for the first time he saw Atropos City laid out before them on the ground.

It was late morning, and the sky was high, and shifted toward the purple spectrum.

Cloud cover was wispy.

The ground below was green and brown, and dark blue across the oceanlike body of water to the west. The settlement itself looked disorderly, but bigger than he had expected. Buildings were made of earthen-colored materials, some even multilevel, some belching smoke. The roads were still dirt, but seemed cleared for the most part. As they flew closer, he could pick out vehicles of various types. The entire thing was clearly rudimentary, but still felt advanced in some odd caveman-in-the-future way.

"Roll dive, Vengeance Two," Jarboe said.

"Roger that," Nimchura replied, twisting the stick and feeling the glorious sense of gravity push him into the seat.

He didn't see the energy ray coming until Jarboe's machine disintegrated in front of his eyes.

"Deuce!" Nimchura screamed as he flew through debris that rattled against the skin of his craft.

He twisted his head left and right, hoping that Jarboe's Firebrand would be beside him, but nothing was left of his wing leader's craft but a scintillating cloud of fire and metal. He pushed the skimmer hard right and peeled off before the U3 targeting system could acquire his signature. The target was below him now, an easy shot.

"Give me a reading, Vengeance One," he said to Jarboe in a voice that was no longer calm.

Still no answer.

He clenched his jaw and rolled into his run at the U3 skimmer base.

He dipped. He jogged left.

He twisted and turned through chaff and another laser blast that would have taken him down if he hadn't grabbed hard air and jaked away at the last moment. He dropped three weapons, and confirmed hits on the laser turret and what appeared to be a hangar. Fire scored the ground. Plasma blasts filled the air with spidery trails of smoke and fire. U3 buildings exploded. To the east, a Quasar made it to the ground, but another exploded in mid drop.

After their second pass, U3 aircraft began to appear in the sky. Probably from *Icarus*, he thought.

His Firebrand had only a few minutes of fuel to spare, so he juked his machine up and hit the solid rockets to engage. His neck snapped back and he nearly blacked out. He started to call Jarboe's name, then felt sick to his stomach. The Z-pads were no match for his Firebrand, though, and he was the best flier still in the sky. It was too easy. Like time came to a stop and the Z-pads just hung in the sky for him. He flamed three before it seemed anything moved.

The sound of the atmosphere scouring his skimmer rose to a scream. His external temp gauges rose again.

He flamed another Z-pod just as it was coming up on a Quasar.

The shuddering of his rocket engines ruddered though his Firebrand. His fuel gauge screamed at him.

It was all up to the rangers, now.

He had to get down.

Nimchura put the Firebrand into a hard dive and hoped that he had enough fuel left to put the son of a bitch down.

A small patch of grassland was available to the southwest. Open, vast enough. He twisted the craft into a line that would get him there. The Taylor part of the T&G engines gave up the ghost then. He yanked the stick hard left to correct for the missing power stream and neared the field.

He was maybe thirty meters off the floor when the Getz part coughed dead.

A Firebrand isn't designed to glide.

There is a feeling of emptiness that is unable to be described.

It is a feeling emptier than lying alone at midnight. Emptier than a dead spacecraft. Emptier than being alone in the dark null-space of gravity where there is no up and no down.

The ground came up hard.

The spacecraft bounced once, then twice. Its left wing clipped a mound, and the Firebrand spun. His voice recorder would later prove that Nimchura screamed, then, but he wouldn't remember it. Nor would he remember the columns of smoke that were rising in the sky above him, or the images of more fighting between Z-pads and Firebrands. Instead, all he could say afterward was that five seconds later everything was done.

That, five seconds later, there was nothing but silence.

That then the wind began to blow over his cracked cockpit and the heat pings started coming from his ship as that same wind cooled the Firebrand's overtaxed engines.

And all he would remember was that he sat there, gripping the Firebrand's joystick in his hands, staring out at the pitted and gored shell of what was left of his Firebrand's crunched-up nose cone, and understanding that those scars came from Jarboe's ship. That the pattern, torn into his craft as he flew through Jarboe's debris, was all that remained of his wing leader.

Nimchura's vision blurred. His chest clutched.

Jarboe was gone.

Nimchura didn't know how long he sat there. All he could say for sure was that the cockpit smelled of sweat, dirt, warm electronics, and cold metal.

He had to do something. Had to get out of here.

He tried to pop the cowling, but the mechanism was stuck. He pounded on the cracked plasteel with his elbow, but that did nothing but bruise him up good.

He pulled his helmet off and pounded it against the cowling.

The first few blows shattered the surface, turning it into a rounded, opaque shell, but leaving it together in its basic shape. It took many more blows before he created an opening that he could focus on. But a few minutes later he had a path out. Fresh air flowed into the cockpit, which he gulped like a parched man at a river.

He unclipped his restraints, climbed his way out of the derelict craft, and found himself surrounded by four members of Universe Three, all with weapons drawn.

On Castles, Balconies, and the Meaning of Life

CHAPTER 33

Atropos
Local Standard Day 249 (ECA 249)
Local Standard Time: 2030 Hours

Sitting on a bench on the rooftop of the building that the colony had taken to calling the Castle, Casmir Francis watched the land around him smolder. The Castle was an adobe brick building, cast from the planet's hard dirt and "finished" only a month prior. It was a simple building, though ostentatious for the moment, a single story shelter, solid and respectable. It protected him and Yvonne from the elements—a fact that had caused the rest of U3's leadership command to prioritize it over his objection. "We've been here long enough," Gregor argued when he formally proposed the build. "We're not going to have our leader die of a cold."

Yvonne hadn't allowed him to say no.

So Universe Three built the house Casmir and Yvonne lived in, and even added the steps up to the rooftop that he was sitting on now, a place that he used so often that he and Yvonne had taken to calling it the balcony.

They had been here a year—or at least a full year for Atropos. It was just under that as Standard Solar Time would measure it, but an Atropos year was just past nine standard months, and its days were just under twenty-eight hours. They had a team working on a calendar, but for now they were still merely counting days.

It was late in the afternoon, growing toward evening.

Another day coming to an end. Day number 249.

The sky was deep purple, streaked with clouds that ran the spectrum of blues and pinks. Thin tendrils of smoke curled from the ground. The odor of charred wood and burnt grasslands had settled over the entire landscape as a sickeningly sharp reminder of the attack from earlier this morning. The action was finished now. They had survived, though many on both sides were killed.

If he tried, he could still smell the exhaust of UG skimmers on the wind.

The damage was mostly under control, but he still wanted to be out there fighting the fires. Dr. Iwal was adamant in his direction to stay out of the smoke, though, and Yvonne made it clear that she would be considerably more than upset if she found him down in the trenches there.

So he sat alone with his hands wrapped around his walking staff, thinking.

They had taken prisoners—eight UG rangers and two pilots—so the next question was going to be how to deal with them.

That was not the question he was thinking about, though, as he sat on the bench atop the Castle and watched his village smolder.

Instead, he was thinking about Ellyn Parker—about Perigee, and the fact that her viewpoint about fighting the UG had been so different from his.

She said real change comes only from inside—that fixing the UG meant actually changing the people. Casmir went a different direction. Get ahead of the process. His approach was to keep UG corporate imperialism from spreading, and then compress it. But as he looked at what remained of what his Universe Three had built and as he smelled the caustic odor of burnt grasses coming from the smoldering remnants of what had been bombed, Casmir understood how wrong he had been.

You cannot stop a tidal wave from flowing over the shore.

Perigee had been right after all.

He coughed hard, though it was more of a psychosomatic reaction.

Footsteps came from behind, but he did not turn.

"The council is here." It was Deidra.

"I will be there shortly. Show them in. Ask your mother to join us."

He sat there for several more minutes.

He was getting old, he thought. Very old.

The Castle had three rooms: a kitchen, a bedroom, and an open-framed great room that they used for most of the leadership team's meetings.

Casmir ambled into the meeting room. Eight members of the team were settled around the table—the rest being up on *Icarus* now, or on *Einstein*, which had been away during the attack. There was so much to do when your entire civilization is starting from scratch.

The team seemed uncomfortable and finicky.

Good for them, he thought as he sat down.

They should be.

Yvonne slipped in from the side door, Deidra just behind.

They were a disheveled lot, most unbathed and still covered in soot and dirt from working all day. Some were bandaged, others merely dirt-streaked. They made him feel useless.

"Where did they come from?" he asked Matt Anderson.

"We don't know for sure, yet," Anderson replied. "But the mission trajectory suggests they have a base somewhere on the second planet of Eta B."

"If that is true," he said. "We will need to confront them now. Do you understand?"

"We're not ready for that, sir," Gregor said. "We don't have the equipment built yet to fight a remote action."

"I don't care," he said. "We can't run anymore. We can't allow them to keep us from making Eta Cassiopeia our home. I'm tired of running. We cannot allow the United Government to have a presence here."

Gregor's gaze let Casmir know that his friend had sensed his change. It was almost surprising that Gregor didn't rise to the comment and force the issue there in front of everyone else. But he didn't. Instead, Casmir's lifelong friend gave him his space. For the moment, anyway.

He took a deep breath.

"This afternoon's events hurt me more deeply than I can

possibly admit," Casmir said. "Like most of you I had convinced myself we were safe. Thank the powers for Gregor's preparations, once again. If the Z-pads had not launched from *Icarus,* we would probably not have survived. We all owe him our lives for his due diligence."

"It is nothing," Gregor said.

"As it is we still have brothers and sisters lying dead. We need to talk about defense," Casmir said. "And by defense, I mean we need to talk about controlling our world, our entire system. And that means dealing with the UG on different terms. I want plans for monitoring every planet in this system. And I want plans for a series of orbiting sensors and weapons that will allow us to protect ourselves at times when *Icarus* or *Einstein* are not here. We need to build more Star Drive craft. We need to grow. But first, I want plans to take out the base that the United Government used to stage this attack. We need to find it, and we need to take it over."

The room was silent, but listening.

"Do you understand?"

The conversation started slowly, but picked up steam as the sky grew dark. By early the next morning, Universe Three had the initial workings of a viable defense strategy.

After the debating was finished, Casmir returned to the balcony to watch Eta Cass rise. He had not slept, of course, and he was feeling numb. It was damp here in the morning, the dew thick from the planet's humidity. It made the mornings an odd combination of sticky, but cool.

"I thought I would find you here," Yvonne said from behind him.

The sound of her footsteps were strong as she walked to his side.

"I like seeing the horizon," he said. "The hills and the sea."

"I know you do."

"They feel quite expansive, don't they?" he said.

They sat together, listening to the wind as it rustled over the fields and the trees, hearing the distant break of waves. Despite the UG attack, those fields were still planted, and the summer should see them yield. They had learned a lot in their first year, though he was sure this coming year would bring new surprises again. Winter would be here soon enough.

Einstein had returned.

In the sky he saw the two Excelsior spacecraft as bright dots that hovered close together like a pair of binary stars. They were still in place, he thought. Still theirs.

He thought about another spacecraft flying outside the Solar System today, *Everguard*, the old UG warhorse that started this whole chain of events when it planted the wormhole pods to begin with, and was now trotting its way back through space at subluminal speeds.

What kind of civilization would those people return to find?

A civilization at war.

That's what they would find. A civilization that would probably always be at war.

Movement came from a field across the way.

It was a beast he had come to call a thunderhoof, stepping out of the woods across the far grassy field. It was a beautiful animal, tall and brown with antlers that rose like a cage over its head.

Casmir reached up and touched Yvonne's shoulder and pointed at the animal with a silent nod. Instinctively, she relaxed into his touch as she peered at it.

It was a painful thing, life.

The battle was over, but the war might never end.

This is the end of

STARBURST

STEALING THE SUN: BOOK 2

If you enjoyed this story, you might be interested in the rest of the series:

STARFALL

STARCLASH

STARBORN

If you enjoyed this story, please consider stopping by your favorite online booksellers' websites and leaving a review. Word of mouth is the most powerful force in the universe when it comes to the livelihood of your favorite authors!

ABOUT THE AUTHOR

Ron Collins is an Amazon best-selling Dark Fantasy author who writes across the spectrum of speculative fiction.

His fantasy series *Saga of the God-Touched Mage* reached #1 on Amazon's bestselling dark fantasy list in the UK and #2 in the US. His short fiction has received a Writers of the Future prize and a CompuServe HOMer Award, and his short story "The White Game" was nominated for the Short Mystery Fiction Society's 2016 Derringer Award.

He has contributed a hundred or so short stories to *Analog*, *Asimov's*, Fiction River Anthology Series, and several other professional magazines and anthologies.

He holds a degree in Mechanical Engineering, and has worked to develop avionics systems, electronics, and information technology before chucking it all to write full-time—which he now does from his home in the shadows of the Santa Catalina Mountains.

Ron's website is: www.typosphere.com
Follow Ron on Twitter: @roncollins13

Sign up for his newsletter to get free stuff!

http://www.typosphere.com/newsletter

ACKNOWLEDGMENTS

I want to thank Nick Kendall and Brigid Collins for their very helpful beta reads in the earliest stages of the work, and then Brigid again for help with identifying important aspects of the story as we were working out back cover stuff. This is an area I always stumble over, and I really appreciated it. In my totally unbiased opinion, the young lady is turning into quite the writer.

I want to thank beta reader extraordinaire Sharon Bass once again for her outstanding help—particularly in this case with a few medical items.

And thanks also goes to Kristine Kathryn Rusch for her kind words about the work that now grace the cover. Kris has always been one of my favorite writers of all time, and to get such support from her is one of those things that makes this writing gig the Coolest Job in the World.

Then, of course, there's always Lisa, who I get to thank both for her outstanding editorial hand, as well as all the other things she brings to my life every day.

I can assure you that any issues that might remain in this work are totally on my shoulders.